ONE-EYED COWBOY WILD

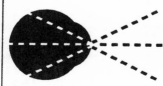

This Large Print Book carries the
Seal of Approval of N.A.V.H.

ONE-EYED COWBOY WILD

John D. Nesbitt

G.K. Hall & Co.
Thorndike, Maine

Published in 1994 by arrangement with Walker Publishing Company, Inc.

All the characters and events portrayed in this work are fictitious.

G.K. Hall Large Print Paperback Collection.

The text of this Large Print edition is unabridged.
Other aspects of the book may vary from the original edition.

Set in 16 pt. News Plantin by Barbara Ingerson.

Printed in the United States on acid-free paper.

Library of Congress Cataloging in Publication Data

Nesbitt, John D.
    One-eyed cowboy wild / John D. Nesbitt.
      p. cm.
    ISBN 0-8161-7477-6 (alk. paper : lg. print)
    1. Cowboys — Wyoming — Fiction. 2. Large type books.
I. Title.
[PS3564.E76O5   1994]
813'.54—dc20   94-26349

for that same pretty girl

CHAPTER 1

Gene Hill would always remember the day his brother Zeke came home from Texas. It was late May on the Wyoming plains — that young and green and hopeful time of year with the promise of warmer weather in the air. Gene felt the sun on his back and the cool breeze on his neck. He was tamping in the corner post when Zeke came riding across the open pasture on his buckskin gelding, wearing a rippling red shirt and a high-crowned white hat. Zeke stood up in the saddle, then stood on the saddle and waved his hat to his brother. The breeze ruffled the full head of black hair as the rider swayed, easy and carefree, on the prancing horse.

Zeke put his hat back onto his head, slid down into the saddle, and kicked the horse into a lope, riding straight at his brother in a drumming gallop. He stopped the horse with its haunches bunching under it, so close that the horse's slobber flicked on Gene's shovel handle. Zeke vaulted off the horse as it stopped, the same old Zeke as always, gliding out of the saddle with both feet clear of the stirrups, pushing himself gently away from the saddle horn, and landing in a perfect walk. He flipped the knotted reins up and over the horse's head to trail on the ground so that Bucky, with a hackamore across his nose but no bit in his mouth, could crop grass.

Gene looked his brother in the eye as Zeke stepped forward with his hand outstretched. They shook, pulled each other close, patted each other on the back, and pushed away. A meadowlark sang *tink-a-link*, the only sound for a moment as the two men stood on the open plain. The blue sky seemed clear and endless, with only a hint of clouds forming on Laramie peak, over Zeke's left shoulder.

Zeke pushed his hat back to let a dark lock of hair fall on his forehead. He squinted and ran the tip of his tongue along his upper lip. "What are you doin' with that post?"

Gene had a wagonload of posts, but he had sunk only the first one into the ground. He said, "Monte sent me out to build a holdin' pen."

Zeke shook his head, then gave a narrow, scolding look he'd copied from their grandmother. "Now, don't go cuttin' this country up into little bitty pieces," he whined.

Gene laughed. "Don't worry. I'm not fixin' to fence in the whole country. Just put in some posts here"— he pointed left, then right — "and there. Then over there . . . and there."

Zeke looked about at the surrounding plains as they rolled away in all directions. "Good a place as any, I guess, if you got to build one." He fished a tobacco sack from his shirt pocket, shook some cheap yellow grains into the tan paper he troughed between his left thumb and forefingers, and pulled the drawstring with his teeth. He offered the pouch to Gene, who shook his head. Grinning broadly, Zeke rolled the cigarette with his left hand, licked it and sealed it, and stuck it in his mouth. He slipped the sack of makings into his pocket and drew out a match, which he flared with his thumbnail and cupped against the breeze, all in one continuous motion.

Gene smiled and nodded. Zeke was always the same, sure and careless. But it was always a surprise to Gene when his brother showed up; Gene never took it for granted that Zeke was still alive. "You just ride in this morning?"

"Just in time for lunch with your new bunkhouse cook." Zeke smiled in obvious self-satisfaction.

"Oh, you met Happy? He's not new. This will be his third year comin' up."

"New to me."

"Did he tell you how to find me?"

"Yeah, he said you'd probably be out here on the end of a shovel, wearin' out the bottoms of your boots instead of the tops."

"I doubt he said the second part."

"I might have added some."

"So, are you just passin' through, or are you thinkin' on stayin' on to work the season?"

"I thought I might ask Monte if he'd put me on."

"There's a lot of work, like this here. Plus we're

puttin' up more and more hay every year, it seems."

Zeke wrinkled his nose.

Gene laughed. "I didn't mean you'd have to blister your hands on a shovel or a pitchfork. It's just that with so much to be done, there might be room for you."

Zeke smiled and nodded. "Well, all right. I'll ask him this evening." He watched as Gene went back to work. "How much of this fence buildin' you think you'll be doin'?"

"Oh, maybe two or three of these pens, a few enclosures for haystacks, I don't know."

"Where's all the posts gonna come from?"

"I expect Monte will send a crew of us up on the mountain to cut a few loads."

"That might be some fun."

"Hate to see you have to use an ax, Zeke."

"Don't worry about me. I bet Bucky and I could keep busy snakin' logs to you, haulin' away snags an' such."

"We'll see what Monte says."

"If he was to put me to work out here with you, that would suit me. I don't know what you think about it."

"All right with me. You and I work together just fine."

"Even though I walked out on you last time?"

"You didn't walk out on me. You just wisely got out of the country before you had to kill Charlie Bickford, that's all. Now you're back, wearin' a pretty red shirt, got fancy taps on your stirrups and probably some new bug in your ass."

"No new bug, Gene."

"Well, Charlie's still workin' here."

"That's what Happy said."

"But he and Jane are split up."

"Uh-huh. I sort of gathered that, but Happy wasn't real thorough on it."

"Maybe six months after you left, she told him it was over."

"Finally saw him for what he is, huh?"

"You'd think so."

"She take up with anyone else?"

"Not in any regular sort of way. She's still young yet, though. I doubt she's much over twenty."

"She's just twenty."

"Well, why am I telling you? You know her, or knew her, better than I did."

"Trouble is, everyone else thought they did, too."

"Charlie Bickford isn't everybody."

"There was his two-bit brother before him."

"Chet?"

"Yeah. Chester."

"Oh, he was just there and gone, just a flash in the pan. I don't think it ever amounted to even half as much as he wanted to let on."

"What's Charlie been up to while I've been gone? He thought he was king coyote when I left."

"Charlie's had a chip on his shoulder the last couple of years."

"Always did."

"Well, it hasn't gotten any better."

"That's the only problem if I go back to work here."

"I doubt it would keep Monte from hirin' you, and I doubt he'd make you work together. Just steer clear of him. I do."

"I won't take any of his hot-jawin'."

"Zeke, you sound like a Texan. And besides, you haven't even been hired yet."

Zeke did get hired that evening, after a short visit with Monte in the foreman's house. He had his bedroll laid out and his ditty bag stowed underneath his bunk in time to answer the supper bell. The evening meal came and went without incident, with Gene seeing to it that he and Zeke sat at the far end of the table from Charlie.

After supper, the ranch hands moved to the living quarters, the section of the bunkhouse that housed their beds, a few chairs, and a stove. It was that time of year when the stove no longer needed to be lit in the evening. The door was open to the outside, letting in the cool evening air and letting out the tobacco smoke. There were no flies yet, none to speak of, so the bunkhouse was a comfy, open, and peaceful place for the time being.

As the punchers lolled in their bunks, Charlie opened it up. "Well, Zeke, what did you learn down there in Texas?"

"Not much."

"That *is* where they say you went, isn't it?"

"That's where I went."

"And did you learn anything?"

"Not much."

"Anything you can tell us about?"

"Since you're so interested, Charlie, I did learn one thing."

"Oh?"

"I learned to like something I didn't care for before."

"What was that?"

"Hot peppers."

"Is that right?"

"Yessir. The old cook liked 'em, so everyone ate 'em and liked 'em."

"Is that right?"

"Yessir, it is. And out of that I learned that you don't always get what you like, but you can learn to like what you get."

"Oh?"

"Or don't get."

"Anything in that for me, Zeke?"

"I doubt it. You asked what I learned, and I told you."

Here it goes, Gene thought. Zeke won't ever back down. Charlie let it pass this time, but he didn't like it.

The next morning, Gene and Zeke drove the wagon out to set more posts, while the other punchers saddled up and headed out to their own jobs on the spread. The climbing sun warmed the morning quickly, taking away the chill of sunrise.

As they rode in the wagon, Zeke said, "Seems like Charlie's workin' the range just east of us. I wouldn't be surprised if he drops by our way sometime today."

"So what if he does?"

"I know he'll try to start something, like he did last night."

"Takes two."

"Uh-huh."

The wagon rumbled on for a while longer until either of them spoke.

"I *am* curious about one thing," Gene said.

"What's that?"

"Did you really acquire a taste for hot peppers?"

"Yes, I did. I got to likin' 'em quite a bit."

"Must take some gettin' used to."

Charlie Bickford did drop by while the brothers were finishing their noonday meal of cold beef and biscuits. Gene had been listening to the song of a meadowlark on the balmy spring air, but the song ended when Charlie rode up. He dismounted and joined them in the shade of the wagon, leaving his horse to graze with the bit in his mouth. After helping himself to a drink from Gene's canteen, he belched, then screwed the cap on. Sitting between the brothers, who were each leaning against a wagon wheel, Charlie gave most of his attention to Zeke. He took his hat off and leaned to set it in front of him; as he did so, Gene saw the beginnings of a bald spot on the back of his head, shining pink and mortal through the red hair.

"Got the makin's, Zeke?" Charlie asked.

Without a word, Zeke fished out the tobacco pouch and tossed it.

"Thanks," Charlie said as he caught it.

Gene watched as the red head bent slightly over

the task of rolling a quirly. He wondered, as he had done in the past, about Charlie's tendency to be in constant motion. The man was never completely still. Sometimes just his head dipped and swayed, ever so slightly, and sometimes, such as when he sat Indian fashion with his spine bent, his whole upper body oscillated. The constant soft, swaying motion, along with the lips frozen in a near smile, gave the impression that Charlie Bickford was forever treasuring a private joke. Gene did not think of him as humorous, but he always had the look about him as if he were onto a pretty good idea and was a little too clever to have to share it.

Gene looked at Zeke, also hatless, who had finished picking his teeth and was balancing the toothpick on his tongue, frisking it through the natural gap between his front teeth. Zeke seemed to be relaxed and genuinely amused. He caught the tobacco sack when it came back, and using both hands, he rolled himself a tight, neat smoke.

Charlie, with the unlit cigarette bobbing in his lips, said, "Can I get a match?"

Zeke tossed a match, and the two men lit up at the same time. "You just carry the habit, nothing else, Charlie?"

Charlie set the match on the grass and dropped a gob of spittle on the warm match head. "I guess you didn't learn much down in Texas. You're still a smart-mouthed little son of a bitch, aren't you?"

"Not so little."

"And not so smart, either."

15

"Charlie, if I'd known how much good will you had to share today, I'd've given you some tobacco this morning so you wouldn't have to ride all the way over here at noontime to bum a smoke."

"You've smoked my tobacco before."

"Sure I have. Smoked your tobacco, drunk your whiskey . . ."

Charlie stopped with the cigarette halfway to his lips. "Go ahead."

"Naw, that's about it."

"Say what you were about to say."

"Nothin' else. That's all I did to anything that was yours." Zeke blew two streams of smoke from his nostrils. "Really yours."

Charlie sprang to his feet, throwing the cigarette onto the ground. "Get up, you son of a bitch, so I can pound you into the dirt."

Zeke rolled to his left and came up dancing, fists dangling.

Charlie, swift and smooth for his bulk, stepped into Zeke and glanced a haymaker off his left cheekbone. Gene could see it was a good punch, from the way Zeke's dark hair flung straight out, but Zeke could take a punch and give one right back, which he did. Then Charlie tried a trick he was known for — faking a left jab and coming up with a left kick. But Zeke had seen the trick before, too, and no doubt had been giving some thought to how he would fight Charlie. He caught Charlie's boot by the back of the heel and jerked the big man to the ground. Then Zeke stood back to let him up, which Gene thought was more quarter than Charlie would have given Zeke.

Charlie rolled over and came up with a shovel in his hands. Gene saw the fun leave Zeke's face, as if his brother were disappointed by the dirty work that the brawl had turned into. Gene couldn't imagine his brother running, but he couldn't imagine him standing up to a shovel, either.

Charlie thrust and feinted with the shovel as Zeke danced and weaved, looking for an opening. Then on a double feint Charlie caught him off balance and came around with the shovel blade, glancing it off Zeke's shoulder and narrowly missing his head. Zeke staggered back, and as Charlie stepped in and drew back for a surer hit, Gene tackled him.

Gene scrambled to his feet and flung the loose shovel away, leaving Charlie to push himself up on all fours. By then Zeke had regained balance, and this time he took his advantage, taking one step forward and kicking Charlie Bickford on the left jaw and cheekbone — not with the full force of premeditation, but with enough force to put the man flat on the ground, with the bald spot shining.

"I hope that's enough," Gene said.

"Enough for me," Zeke added. "How about you, Charlie?"

Charlie pushed himself up to his knees. "Yeah. Just plenty." Then he got to his feet, found his hat, and walked unevenly to his horse. He pulled himself into the saddle and reined around, eyes flashing hatred at Gene and Zeke as he spoke to both of them. "We'll fight again, I know that. I know I can whip you by yourself, Zeke, but if you think you need your brother to help, why, I can bring one, too. He's not so far off I can't send for him. Man on man is more to my likin', but you want to fight brothers against brothers, why we can do that too, by God." Then he kicked his horse and they were gone.

Charlie was gone, but Gene still had a sense of him, the taste of dirt in his mouth, the smell in his nostrils, the live man-smell of warmth and sweat, leather, cloth, and dust.

While Gene stomped out the two cigarette stubs that had fallen in the fray, Zeke picked up his hat and dusted off the underside of the brim, then put it on his head. He held his right hand in front of him, opening and closing the fist as if to check for damages. Then he looked at the retreating horse and rider and said in a mocking tone, "Well, by God, I suppose we can."

CHAPTER 2

Gene Hill counted Owen Pollard, the cook who went by the name of Happy, among his best friends at this point in life. This man, a good fifteen years older than Gene, was not a likely candidate for a cowboy's sidekick. Happy was in his early forties, a quiet, reserved man, educated and obviously not a native of the plains. He was solid, but he did not have the lean, weathered toughness of a ranch hand. An able rider and a good man with an ax, he nevertheless looked most natural in an apron, which seemed in tune with his wire-rimmed spectacles and his almost colorless hair, thinning on top but lying thick on the sides and neck, pale as winter grass or dried corn silk.

He came by his name through the same vein of humor by which large men come to be called Tiny. But even though he was not bubbly, he was not a sourpuss either. Gene knew him as a shrewd observer of life around him, a man with a dry sense of humor. From a spare remark dropped here or there, Gene understood that Happy had been disappointed by a woman earlier in life and was not anxious to set himself up for another letdown. Apparently content to remain single, Happy was the kind of man who might have become a sheepherder or a miner, except that he genuinely liked cooking and the company of others.

Gene and Happy had been friends from the start, each having discovered in the other someone to share the wry observations they drew from daily life. Gene's uppermost interests were women, the land, and cattle, in that order; Happy's were books, personal histories, and recipes, in that order. But they both liked the exchange of ideas, and so they had whiled away many a winter night in wandering conversation as the rest of the bunkhouse hands tossed poker chips and genial insults.

Gene and Happy sat on the back steps outside the kitchen at the far end of the building from the living quarters, where the other men were lounging. Gene told Happy about the fight that had taken place that day.

"Sounds like this is just the beginning," Happy said.

"I think so."

Happy lit his pipe. "It seems like this might put you in a tight spot, sooner or later."

Gene began cleaning his fingernails with his jackknife as Happy fussed with his pipe, tamping and relighting it. Now that it had been said out loud, Gene saw it even more clearly. Here he was, past twenty-five and looking at thirty, with life just beginning to look like a trail that had some direction. Farther down that trail he saw himself matched with a good woman, settled on their own place, with livestock of their own. A fellow wouldn't want to be always looking over his shoulder. "I'm not really worried about that, but I agree," he said. "I can't help worrying about Zeke, though, and how tight a spot he might get himself into."

"You do have to worry about him, I guess. He's your little brother."

"He just acts younger. Actually, Zeke's older."

"Oh, really? I thought it was the other way around."

"No, he's older. But I still worry about him."

"I doubt you need any advice on how you should keep from getting all caught up in his troubles yourself."

"I sort of stepped into it today."

"Oh, that much shouldn't be trouble."

"What should be?"

"What could grow out of it." Happy put another match to his pipe. "I don't know your brother like you do, of course, but he strikes me as the kind that can end up with the law after him."

Gene nodded. For a long time he had sensed in his brother a wild streak, a lawlessness, that he didn't find in himself.

Happy went on. "Has he said anything about why he came back from Texas?"

"No, not to me. He just showed up. You think he got into trouble down there?"

"I'm not saying it definitely, but he's not here to stay, is he? Not like you, I mean."

"No, not forever. He'll probably move on at some time or another."

"When he does, he may or may not have the

law interested in him. And you'll be the one left behind." Happy blew a cloud of smoke at a small fly.

"I see what you mean."

"None of my business, of course."

"Of course, but I appreciate it." Gene closed his knife and put it in his pocket. "I know how to keep out of trouble with the law, myself, but I appreciate the warning." Gene nodded as he saw the possibilities laid out before him. "You're right," he continued. "This feud Zeke is into wouldn't end up with just a night in the crowbar hotel. It can go farther than that, and Wyoming is a bona fide state now, with laws and all."

"Besides," Happy said, smiling, "you've got prettier things to worry about."

Gene looked off to his left into the still-warm evening sun, and smiled. Even if Happy wasn't a woman chaser himself, he had a well-wishing interest in Gene's amours. "That reminds me," Gene said. "I have a little favor to ask."

"Expert advice to the lovelorn?"

"No, but close. An apple pie."

"What?"

"I'd like to set up a little picnic Sunday afternoon for Ginny and me. I thought I'd ask her to see if Jane can come, and I'll bring Zeke along for a sheepdog."

"Or wolf."

"Or wolf." Gene laughed.

"And you'd like my humble self along to act as chaperon and to add dignity to the affair?"

"That's right. And I thought while we were at it, we could cut you a wagonload of stove wood."

"That sounds cordial. Invite me along on a gala social event, and then send me off to chop wood."

"Zeke and I can do our share of the wood choppin'."

"Sounds like you have this pretty well planned."

"I've given it some thought."

"And all I have to do is bake a pie, an apple pie."

"Oh, you might pack along a few steaks, a spud or two, and anything else that might come to mind."

"I see. You *have* given it some thought." Happy paused. "By the way, was any of this your brother's idea?"

Gene smiled. "It did come out of a conversation between the two of us."

The next evening, after bolting his supper and giving himself a fast scrub-down, Gene took a brisk ride into town. Of the two young women Gene saw as candidates to share his future, one was Virginia Bransford. At the age of twenty-two, having returned from two years of schooling, Ginny lived with her parents and brother in their two-story frame house in town.

Her father, William, operated a general store, which also employed Ginny's brother, Henry. Midway between Ginny's age and Gene's, Henry was born and raised to town ways — always a clean shirt and collar, always a smile and a clear eye, always a handshake. As yet unmarried and clearly an eligible bachelor, he read current books of philosophy and science in order to broaden his knowledge of the world, and he took a special interest in the invention called the telephone, which he had seen demonstrated in Laramie and Cheyenne. Gene imagined that in Henry's version of what the future looked like, there was a woman and a painted house, but in the foreground there was probably a bank, made of quarried stone, with lettering on an arched window reading "Henry Bransford, Pres."

Henry answered the door and invited Gene into the sitting room. Gene stood, hat in hand, as Henry went to tell Ginny she had a visitor. As Gene looked around the room and noticed the rosewood bureau, the mantel clock, and the gilt-edged photographs, he wondered again how his life might match with hers — would his ways change toward hers, would it be the other way around, or would there be a common hearth somewhere between the sheet-metal stove and the stone fireplace?

"Hello, Gene. What a surprise!" Ginny's voice was musical as she glided into the sitting room and gave Gene her hand.

He took her four fingers in his, pressed them with his thumb, and released her, but not before he caught the faint smell of perfume. His hand felt clean from having touched hers.

"Won't you sit down?" she offered as she smoothed her dress and took one end of the sofa.

"Thank you," he answered, taking a wooden armchair he had already picked out.

Henry came back into the room and seated himself in the stuffed armchair in the corner by the fireplace, as far as he could get from the scene of courtship and still be in the same room. Lighting a lamp, he took up a book from the low table beside him and began reading.

Ginny's hair looked freshly washed, as it always did, shining in the lamplight as it fell in yellow waves to her shoulders. Her blue eyes sparkled as she looked at Gene and said, "It's certainly nice to see you. I wasn't expecting you." Her hands lay neatly joined in her lap.

Gene smiled, appreciating her neatness — neatness in manner, neatness in appearance. She might not have been expecting anybody in particular, but he doubted that she spent much of her waking day unprepared. "I just rode in on a short visit," he said.

She nodded, as she had no doubt learned to nod, to help young men through their nervousness.

He said the words as he had sketched them out in his mind. "I was wondering what you might think of a little outing — a picnic — on Sunday afternoon."

"Where did you have in mind?"

"Out our way," he said, hesitating.

She nodded.

"I thought maybe a few of us could go along. I invited Happy, our cook, and he seems agreeable to putting on a little cookout if we help him get a wagonload of stove wood up on Brush Creek."

"It sounds as if you have it well organized. Who

else is on your guest list?"

"You, of course."

"Yes." She smiled broadly.

"And I was wondering if you were still good friends with Jane Carling."

"Jane? Of course. We see each other every day." Then she looked curiously at Gene. "Does Happy have . . . something like an interest in Jane?"

"Oh, no," he said quickly, "I was also plannin' to invite my brother, Zeke."

"Oh." The syllable seemed very noncommittal. Then she said, "I heard he was back."

"He got back a few days ago, and he's workin' with me out on the Redboot."

"And I assume he has an interest in Jane." She laughed.

"More so than Happy."

"Well, Gene, it all sounds fine to me. I'll have to talk it over with Jane, of course."

"I was hoping you would. That way it would be easier for her to say no if she didn't think it was a good idea."

"I'm pleased that you place that kind of trust in me, Gene. I can talk to her about it in the morning." Then, after a pause, she said, "Wasn't there some kind of trouble before he went away?"

Gene sensed an invitation to explain. "Yes, there was. That was at about the time you went away to school."

She nodded.

"Well, Zeke was interested in Jane. So was Charlie Bickford. And Charlie, the way I see it, anyway,

26

was a faster talker and got her to say she'd marry him."

"That didn't last very long, really."

"No, it didn't, but in the meanwhile, Zeke and Charlie couldn't be anywhere near each other without the sparks flyin'."

"Was that it?"

"Well, I think Zeke tried to talk Jane out of it, and I think Charlie threatened to kill Zeke, but" — he smiled — "nothing that turned into outcomes."

As Ginny nodded, it seemed to Gene that she turned her thoughts inward, comparing what she had just heard to what she might have heard from others, Jane included. Then she looked at Gene and asked, "Did he come back to see her?"

"I don't think so. I think he thought she was married and everything was blown over." He paused, then went on. "He just came back on his own, as nearly as I know."

"Well, let's see how we can do this. I can talk to Jane tomorrow, and if you don't hear from me to the contrary, you can plan on it."

"I could ride back in tomorrow evening —"

"Oh, let's not make anyone make an extra trip. I could send a message out to the affirmative, also, but either way would be an extra trip. Henry," she said raising her voice, "you'll run a message out to Redboot for me if I need it, won't you?"

Henry, who no doubt had followed every word, looked up from the book that had absorbed him. "Oh, sure."

"I doubt that it will be necessary, but that is probably the simplest way."

"I'll keep the evening open," Henry said, with a smile and a flick of the eyebrows, as he went back to his book.

"Now for the next part," Gene said. As he spoke, he became aware of the smell of the kerosene lamp.

"And what's that?" she asked, smiling and re-folding her hands in her lap.

"Would you like me to come pick you up? I can get the use of the wagon."

She almost grimaced. "That would mean two trips for you."

Yes, he thought, sitting next to you all the way.

"Let me see what Henry thinks. Henry . . ."

"Yes?"

"What would you think of driving Jane and me out to Redboot on Sunday afternoon if we don't need you to ride there tomorrow evening?"

That was it. It was the comfort, not the company. She would simply rather ride in Henry's buggy than in the ranch wagon. Gene couldn't blame her.

"Sounds like I'm going there one way or the other," Henry said, smiling the banker's smile.

"You're certainly welcome to join us," Gene offered.

"Actually," Henry said, pursing his lips, "I need to get out that way to see old Walter Rose. I could drop you off, go talk to him, and come back to pick you up. It wouldn't be much out of my way." He looked back at his book.

"Henry," she said, "do I sense that you might try to catch a peek at his daughter?"

"Probably not," he answered, not even looking up from his book. "Walter trains good harness horses, and I need to be bringing along another buggy horse. Caesar is going to start showing his age before long."

Riding home, Gene took it slower than he did on the way into town, but he still kept a brisk pace, hoping to be in his bunk by midnight. The night was cool and semi-dark, and he had his jacket buttoned up. As he rode he relived the bright, pleasant scene in the Bransford sitting room. Then it occurred to him that every time he had seen Virginia Bransford they had been indoors — at the dance, at the church social, and half a dozen times in her parents' house. That would change Sunday when he would see her in a new setting.

Gene slowed the horse and angled it as the trail dropped down and across a dry wash, then he let the horse have rein again as it scrambled back up onto the level. A quarter mile further he slowed the horse to a stop. The half-moon lit up the prairie well enough that he could see a ribbon of wagon track heading south. Down that road, sleeping peacefully in the dark, he hoped, lived Katharine Rose. Hers was the other face that sometimes appeared at the door of that cabin a little farther down life's trail.

CHAPTER 3

No news was good news. Henry did not show up at the bunkhouse on Thursday night, which meant that the picnic would go as planned. That was good news; Ginny was interested enough to ride all the way out for the event. It also occurred to Gene that she might have discouraged him from a second ride into town because she expected some other caller. Well, no matter — she was coming out on Sunday.

It amused him to think of how ready she was to use her brother as her personal telephone. Then it amused him less to realize that at some time Sunday, Henry might mention to Katharine Rose that Gene and Zeke were entertaining Ginny and Jane. Well, no matter there either — there was no need to be sly, and there was no such thing as a secret in this country anyway. Gene nodded to himself at that thought.

There were certainly no secrets in the bunkhouse. The men played cards at the table where they ate, in the middle room of the long building, between the kitchen and the sleeping quarters. It was custom to have a poker game on Saturday night, unless too many of them decided to go to town. A fellow's life was generally an open book in the bunkhouse — at least his current day-to-day life was — and it was even more so at the poker table.

There, the small talk served its various purposes of making noise, camouflaging a move, prodding the other player, and keeping up the happy spirit of the game. On this Saturday night, plenty of good-natured remarks were passed on the subject of the next day's picnic.

Zeke and Gene took the ribbing in the same spirit, but Charlie remained in a sullen mood. Neither he nor the brothers had brought up the fight since the afternoon it happened, but anyone in the room could tell there was bad blood among them. Charlie glowered from behind the bruise on his cheekbone, while Zeke pretended to be polite to him, and Gene ignored him. At one point, when Pete Bonair, a puncher and bronc twister from up Montana, was talking pitty-patter about how careful a man should be around them green-broke fillies, Charlie had enough. He slapped his cards down on the table, sprang up and kicked his chair away, slammed his hat on his head, and stomped out.

"Mad 'cause he don't get no pie," said Rusty George.

"He could have some pie," Bonair said. "Happy made a pie for us too."

"I guess we can cash him in, and leave his change on his bunk, eh, fellows," offered Jack Townsend, who acted as banker for their games.

There was a general mutter of agreement, so Jack cashed out Charlie's remaining chips and left a small pile of coins on his bunk in the next room. The game rolled right along, dealer's choice, for a few more minutes without much talk, until the evening air carried the sound of a horse walking across the hard-packed ranch yard and then breaking into a gallop.

Relief seemed to settle on the bunkhouse as Pete Bonair said, "Good night to stay out of the bar-rooms."

"I hope he cuts his wolf loose but good before he comes back," Rusty George said.

"Yeah," Jack Townsend added, "he's been a real piss-pot lately."

Sunday morning, there was no sign yet of Charlie Bickford, and the little pile of coins lay untouched on his bunk.

Gene and Zeke, having bathed the night before, shaved and spruced up. Happy sat by watching, smoking his pipe in what seemed to be wry amusement.

"You boys are gonna be a pretty pair," he said, "a pretty pair to draw to."

Rusty George, who was sitting nearby in the light of the open door and doing violence to a pair of Levi's with a needle and thread, said, "Trouble is, them two angels from town might come out here, eat your apple pie, then take a notion to discard and draw again."

Zeke screwed his mouth to the right, stretching his left cheek for the razor. "I think Jane already did that once — discarded, anyway. Knew a bad card when she saw it. Picked him off like a dirty deuce in a new deck."

Gene looked at his brother. Sometimes he envied Zeke's downright nerve, but at times like this, when the self-assurance ran too strong, he disliked his brother, or at least disliked his gloating. It was on the tip of his tongue to tell Zeke he should take warning himself if he thought Jane knew a bad card when she saw it. Instead he just said, "I watched Zeke buy a pot last night."

"Which time?" Rusty George asked.

"When he drew to an inside straight, bet it like three aces with a kicker, and then ran it through like he'd hit a full house."

Rusty paused in his tailoring. "Did you do that, Zeke?"

Zeke continued to glow. Not indicating clearly whether he was answering Rusty's tease, he rubbed the back of his left hand on the freshly shaven cheek. "Just as smooth as a baby's ass," he said.

The boys had the team hitched up and their horses saddled and had been fidgeting for an hour when Henry's buggy came wheeling over a rise, sending up a thin cloud of dust against the blue sky. Henry looked stylish. He was neatly dressed as always, flanked by two pretty girls, and drawn by a high-stepping bay with four white socks.

"Well, here comes Henry with the goods," Happy said.

Zeke pushed back his hat. "Don't he always look

like he just cut a fat hog in the ass?"

Gene had had enough. He would take this one chance to put a tie-down on Zeke before the picnic got under way. "Zeke," he said, "why do you have to talk like a Texan?"

"What's wrong with that? Half the people in this country are from Texas anyway."

Gene felt a flush of anger. "Yeah," he said. "The Bickfords, for example."

Henry handed the ladies down from the buggy and shook hands around. He confirmed his earlier plan to drive over to see Walter Rose.

"You're welcome to come along with us," Happy said.

"Nah, you don't need me, and I've been wanting to see Walter anyway. This is a good chance."

"I made a pie," Happy said, "and I plan to cut it in six pieces — or maybe one of these ladies will."

"Doesn't look like mine today, Happy, but thanks all the same." Henry pulled himself up into the buggy.

"Just remember I asked. Now I'll have to let one of the brothers eat it."

Henry laughed lightly, bid them a good afternoon, and drove away.

Jane turned to Zeke. "It's nice to see you again, Zeke. Welcome back."

Zeke smiled, looked halfway down to his boots, and looked back up at her. "Nice to be welcome. And good to see you, of course."

"Are you here for the season, or do you think you'll stay?"

If Zeke had been sheepish for a moment, it wasn't for long. "Depends on how I get treated," he said, "but I doubt I'll get run off very easy."

Jane deflected the remark by turning and saying, "Did you hear that, Happy? I can't tell if it's a threat or a plea."

Happy brightened at Jane's conversation. "I only know one way to get at a fellow," he said, "but between the two of us, we could put the squeeze on him. I say we go easy on him, for the time being at least."

Jane laughed, but she said nothing.

Virginia looked across at Gene as the group stood there in the ranch yard, and she said, "You couldn't have picked a prettier day, Gene."

He wanted to say, "Or a prettier girl," but he simply said, "I was hoping it would be nice, and it turned out fine."

On the procession to Brush Creek, Happy drove the wagon carrying the two girls, the picnic food wrapped in a canvas, the pie protected in a hat box, and the woodcutting tools. Gene rode along on the left side of the wagon while Zeke rode on the right. It was a fresh afternoon on the greening prairie, sunny but not hot, with the smell of new grass in the air.

Gene looked at Zeke, then at Happy, then at the two pretty women. This was what made life good, he thought — kinship, friendship, companionship. Gene realized that he was in the prime of life, young enough for optimism, old enough for caution. On a day like today, life stretched out open and free like the country, with no tangles in sight. This was the time people lived for, he thought, and if a man could be aware of the time when it was his, then the prime of life was even richer.

Brush Creek ran a trickle of water year round, and so it held some favored picnic spots. Happy drove to one where there was a spreading cottonwood for shade and an established campfire pit made of rocks from the creek bed. The three men had agreed ahead of time that Happy would start a fire, then entertain the two ladies as they rested from their travel, while Gene and Zeke piled the wagon with stove wood. For that purpose, Happy had brought along a volume of Robert Louis Stevenson, from which he would read aloud to the two ladies.

The wood-gathering itself did not figure to be a big chore. Gene and Zeke intended to load the wagon with pieces five or six feet long, to be cut into stove lengths back at the ranch. The wagon would fill up fast and yet make a decent showing for the afternoon's effort. Zeke roped and dragged the deadfall out to open spots, where Gene, swinging a double-bit ax, trimmed and sized the logs. They had brought along a buck saw, but their system worked well enough that they stayed with the smaller diameters and had a wagonload in a little over an hour.

When Gene drove the wagon back to the picnic spot, he heard the rhythms of Happy's elocution before he saw anybody. Then he rounded a knoll and saw Happy standing with his text, the women seated side by side on a canvas, and further back in the shade, seated on his horse, Charlie Bickford.

Happy and his intended audience seemed to be oblivious to their visitor, but as the wagon creaked closer and Happy looked his way, Gene read the warning on his face. Licking the dust from his lips, Gene looked back at Zeke, who was poking along behind and slapping the knotted end of his rope against his leg. Gene caught Zeke's eye and motioned with his head toward the picnic spot. Zeke looked and then, with downturned mouth and rolling eyes, showed that he was ready to be tolerant.

Happy drew his reading to a close as Gene and Zeke drew up. Ginny and Jane rewarded the cook with a small round of applause and smiling compliments.

Charlie, who presumably had not been there long, stepped off his horse and dropped the reins to let it graze.

Gene, climbing down from the wagon box, said, "Afternoon, Charlie."

Charlie nodded to Gene and then to Zeke, who said nothing. Then Charlie spoke to Happy, as if the cook had been in charge of the whole affair. "Well, Happy, I just happened to be riding by, and it sounded like somebody down here was cryin' for help. Then I see you have these two ladies spellbound." He turned to the women and tipped his hat, and they returned what in Gene's view looked like forced smiles. Then, back to

Happy, he said, "Now that I see everybody's safe, maybe I should just move along and not crowd anybody's company." But he just stood there.

"You don't need to be in any hurry, Charlie," said the cook, following the form of cow-camp hospitality. "I'm about ready to sizzle some steaks, and I suppose we have enough for a sixth person."

"If it's not any trouble."

"Oh, no," Happy said, in a deadpan tone that left the door open either way.

"It's all company grub anyway," Charlie said, in what served for him as humor. He looked again at the women, whose smiles seemed to Gene to be pained.

Gene was reminded of how irritating Charlie could be. The man always seemed to want to control any gathering he was part of, even when he met with halfhearted courtesy. At the moment, he seemed to want to push the women into speaking to him.

"Hello, Virginia. Afternoon, Jenny."

Virginia just said hello in return, with no change in composure, but Jane flushed at the use of her nickname. The formal tone of her voice as she said "Good afternoon, Mr. Bickford" should have had the effect of a bucket of cold water, but all it got was a smile.

Gene watched as Charlie rolled a log around so that he could sit near the women, with his bruised left cheek away from them. Gene smiled to see that the maneuver caused Charlie to sit next to Virginia instead of Jane. Then, as an apparent gesture of gallantry, Charlie took off his hat and set it, underside up, on the log between himself and Virginia. That seemed to tell Gene to sit elsewhere, and there was no easy way to do otherwise. Gene stood and waited until Zeke sat on the ground a little to Jane's right. Gene completed a semicircle by sitting at Zeke's right.

Gene didn't like the arrangement, partly because it was forced. As soon as he sat down, he wanted to get up. "Do you need anything, Happy?" he asked. "Could you use a hand?"

"I'm fine. I put the potatoes in the coals a little while ago, and I'm just about ready to slap the steaks on." Happy had brought along a wire grate, which he was rubbing with a piece of beef fat.

Gene got out a canteen and tin cups, in deference to the ladies, and poured water. He poured himself a second drink, and one for Zeke; the women barely sipped, and Charlie waved him off with a hand.

The group was silent for a full two minutes, until Charlie spoke. "Flies already," he said, shooing a fly that was buzzing between him and Virginia.

"Wonder what draws 'em," Zeke tossed out.

Gene thought he saw a trace of a smile on the women's faces until Charlie answered.

"You know what they say. A fly's just as happy whether he lights on a pot of honey or on a cow pie."

This time it was Ginny's turn to redden, from her blond hairline down to the collar of her white

39

blouse. Gene looked from her to Jane, whose face had hardened. It was clear that neither woman was going to speak at that point.

Gene looked over at the fire pit, where wisps of smoke were rising around the sizzling steaks. He smiled at Happy, who smiled back. Then Gene pushed his hat back and wiped his forehead with the back of his hand. "I'm glad we got the firewood cut and done with."

Ginny looked over at the wagon, then smiled at Gene. "It looks like you did well," she said, as if she was really interested in firewood and talked about it every day.

"Oh, yeah," Zeke spoke up. "Gene's a real hand with an ax."

"Probably good with a broom, too," Charlie said, spitting off to his left.

Ginny and Jane looked at each other, expressionless, as if to say, "See?"

Then Zeke, on the heels of Charlie's sneering comment, said, "Or a shovel."

The atmosphere went dead. Charlie looked down at his empty hat where it lay upside down between him and Ginny. She and Jane looked at each other again. Zeke looked at the little heap of dirt he was digging in front of him with a stick.

Gene, as he glanced from one to the other, felt powerless to change the downhill drag of the picnic. He had been hoping the event would pick things up between him and Ginny, but it seemed to be having the opposite effect. He could tell she wasn't enjoying herself, and he felt as if he was to blame. If she was disgusted by Charlie, all the better, but if she was irritated at Zeke, she might be less willing to have that much to do with Gene.

He couldn't blame her if she felt that way, but Zeke was, after all, his brother. Nothing would change that.

Charlie spoke up. "I think I'll have a drink of water after all." He pushed himself up from his seat on the log and, looking past Virginia, said, "Jane, can I get you anything?"

She looked up at him where he stood, and she seemed relieved at the name he had used. "No, thank you, Charlie," she said.

Gene looked at Ginny, widening his brows to form a question.

She smiled and said, "No, thanks."

After a moment, Zeke spoke. "I'll tell you what," he said, looking at Jane. "I wish we'd brought along some lemonade. I wish I'd thought of it earlier."

"It's all right," she said back. "This is fine."

"Maybe next time," Zeke offered.

"Yes, maybe next time," Jane said, smiling as if to say it was a nice thing to talk about.

Before long, Happy dug the potatoes out of the coals and took the steaks off the grate. As the picnickers all bent to their plates, Gene took the opportunity to observe Charlie. It seemed that with Zeke's return, Charlie was tossing his hat back in the ring as a rival, too stubborn to admit what he had been told earlier. Gene remembered a story about Charlie, that he had defended himself in court one time, in Texas, and he had won his case. The memory of that story helped Gene define Charlie — self-assured, confident. Gene watched the red head bent over the plate, with the bald spot showing. Charlie raised his head to observe Jane and then Virginia, all the while chewing slowly, the stubbled jaws bulging at the hinges, the head in its constant swaying motion. It was clear to Gene that Charlie did not see himself as others did. He saw himself as a worthy suitor to a woman who had already turned him away; he considered himself deserving of a good woman in a land where everyone had a new chance and was supposed to be equal. All he had to do was give it his best fight, and he would win. Gene read in Charlie's faint smile and waggling head a sense of self-confidence that was undeserved.

Gene, working on his own plate but taking glances in between bites, turned his thoughts to Zeke. This was his only brother, his only living family. Earlier in life, as they were growing up, Gene had felt an identity with his brother. But somewhere along the way, maybe in Zeke's trip to Texas and back, Gene had come to realize there were some parts of Zeke that were only Zeke, just as there were some parts of himself that weren't in his brother. Things did not flow as freely between them as they once seemed to.

Partly through Happy's remarks, Gene had come to accept the idea that Zeke had a germ of corruption in him. It wasn't just his reckless, impulsive nature that had always been in contrast with Gene's restrained nature. There was also something deep down, a basic disregard for rules. Zeke liked to win, and he usually did. Like Charlie, he had vast faith in himself and his abilities, but unlike Charlie, and to Zeke's credit, he had a carefree nonchalance about him that made him seem more acceptable. Gene did not totally identify with his brother, but he knew him from the inside. He knew that Zeke's belief in himself was intertwined with his belief in his own good luck, which kept him from being too arrogant.

Gene took a sip of water, and he felt his lips leave a smudge of grease on the cool tin cup. He had the sense of things fitting into place. He knew that life's trail leads only in one direction, and once a thing is done or known, it can't be undone or unknown. Today he had placed his brother somewhere in between himself and Charlie Bickford, a man he despised, and he could not go back on that thought. He had also seen that there might be a gulf between Ginny and himself, one that would keep them from coming closer together. These were not easy thoughts on his mind as he mopped his tin plate with biscuit, but he knew they would stay.

Happy scraped the plates into the fire and wiped them clean, fairly clean, with a linen cloth he had brought along in the camp kit. Still playing the gracious host, he included Charlie in what was to be the crowning touch.

"Charlie, you solved the problem of what I was going to do with the extra piece of pie."

A smile came onto the swaying face, a smile that said things come my way. "It wouldn't be good manners to turn you down," he said.

At the mention of good manners, Virginia, who had been the perfect picture of self-restraint all afternoon, arched her eyebrows. Gene caught it and she saw him catching it, and her eyes twinkled as she smiled faintly at him. The look of recognition helped him keep from bursting out laughing, and he sensed, in that moment, that all was not lost between them.

CHAPTER 4

Monte, the foreman, kept his finger on the pulse of Redboot well enough to know there was bad blood between Zeke and Charlie, and he managed to send them out on jobs that had a healthy chunk of country in between. None of the hands knew for sure what went on in the shrewd foreman's head. Gene imagined that Monte wanted to keep the brothers working together, because Gene tended to keep his brother in line.

Gene recalled a trapper who had passed through the country one autumn. Gene had crossed paths with him for just a few minutes, but the man had left an impression. Clean-shaven and rosy-faced, he was not the image of the old mountain man. His clothes were clean and in good repair, as was the outfit on his packhorse. He carried both a shotgun and a rifle for saddle guns. He was on his way to Douglas to trap and kill coyotes, bobcats, badgers, porcupines, and mountain lions — all for a bounty, and any pelts would be his. He was going to work for a couple of big outfits up that way. He was a thoroughly pleasant man, but he had the cold air of a professional killer. What Gene remembered about him now was his dogs. He had a pack of about six dogs, all middle-sized, of various and mixed breeds. Two of the dogs were harnessed together and joined by a six-inch length of chain links and swivels. One dog looked to be a beagle, with maybe some trace of a terrier that had jumped a fence, while the other dog had to be at least half coyote. As they talked, the trapper told Gene that the wild-looking dog was half coyote, and the smaller dog kept it in check. Gene was impressed with the whole incident — the trapper's friendliness, his cool control, the harnessed dogs.

On Monday morning, Monte sent Charlie south to ride line for a week, and he sent Gene and Zeke north to bring in dry cows that hadn't calved that spring.

The plan was for the brothers to be out three days, making two night camps in the open. They were to cut out and gather the dry cows and bring them to headquarters so they could be pushed out to the hardscrabble range to the south. Any that didn't take the bull the next time would be shipped or beefed on the spot.

Meanwhile, Gene thought, it wouldn't be long before Monte had a crew pushing the pairs up to summer range. From the foreman's point of view it ought to be a good place to stick either Charlie or the two brothers. Gene liked it on the mountain, and he thought it would be all right if he and Zeke were sent there. It was just as likely that Monte would keep Gene and Zeke at the odd jobs, such as building fences, cutting fence posts, and, later in the season, cutting hay. But there was no point in trying to second-guess Monte or in making suggestions. Once, in his first year, when Gene had tired of alkali dust on the flat and had a yearning to wash his face in a mountain stream, he had asked the boss when he might get to go to the mountain. "When I say so" was the answer, and Monte didn't get around to saying so until the next summer. For the present, then, Gene was on a three-day job and would take whatever came next.

Gene and Zeke rode out from headquarters that Monday morning as the sun was lifting in the east. Gene could smell dust and sagebrush on the cool morning air. That, and the sound of two horses picking up a good walk on a worn trail, gave him a feeling that the week was starting out fine, in spite of how things had gone the day before.

As soon as they were well away from the ranch buildings and satisfied that Charlie was long gone in the opposite direction, Gene brought up the subject of Sunday's picnic.

"Well, what did you think of the way yesterday's little affair went?"

"Couldn've been worse."

"How?"

"Charlie could've brought his brother."

Gene laughed. "He sure put a damper on the whole event, didn't he?"

"That he did."

"I barely got a chance to say three words to Ginny. Looked like you didn't do any better."

Zeke shrugged. "I doubt I did. She seemed stiff as a board, and I wasn't what you might call at ease."

"That's how it looked to me."

"But I got the general impression Jane wouldn't mind seeing me again."

"Her even agreeing to go along to begin with was a good sign, seems to me."

"Oh, yeah. Even more so for your gal."

"Don't know if I could call her my gal, but yeah, it all looked pretty good at the start."

"Then things went downhill."

"Yep." Gene straightened his reins and then said, "But I didn't get the feelin' I was completely off the list when all was said and done."

"For you, it could be good either way. I imagine you'll be wantin' to get out there to old Walter Rose's place, to see what kind of draft horses he's bringin' along."

"I have to admit to an interest in that direction."

Zeke, who had been slapping his leg with his rope end, touched spurs to his horse. "Hep ha, Bucky, let's pick it up."

"Hep ha, Dodger," Gene said, and the horse took off after the other, following it at half a length as the two pair loped gently across the prairie morning.

They made it to the north range by late morning, and by late afternoon they had cut out fifteen head and brought them to water. That evening, with the cows bedded down and the horses picketed, as Gene squatted on his heels to build the fire, he said, "I think we got the easiest part done."

Zeke, sitting Indian fashion and rolling a smoke, said, "You're probably right. It'll probably take us all day to get another half dozen head outa them headers."

"You call 'em headers. You're talkin' about the draws, uh?"

"What's wrong with what I call 'em?"

"Nothin'. Pete Bonair calls 'em breaks. And coulees. All the same. Good hidin' place for cows."

Zeke smiled as he flipped the cigarette into his mouth. "We'll get 'em," he said as he popped a match.

Gene looked at his brother so pleased at himself, and he smiled back. "Oh, yeah, we'll get 'em."

The next morning they were up with the dawn, drinking their second cup of coffee as Zeke watered the horses and Gene broke camp. Not wasting time, they saddled up and headed for the rough country. By midmorning they had hazed three fat dry cows down onto the plain.

Zeke held his hat as he dragged his shirt cuff across his brow. "This is rougher country than it looks. If a cow had a mind to, she could play hide and seek from now till breakfast."

Gene nodded and took a drink from his canteen. "No way of knowin' if we'll get 'em all, or when."

"I 'magine we'll know when it's time to call it good."

"I 'magine."

They rode up a wide draw until it split, fingering off into what would obviously become two separate mazes. Once into the ravines, the riders lost track of each other. It had been that way all morning, except when both of them happened to be up on spines at the same time. The spines or ridges were mostly dry, crumbly soil, supporting sagebrush and soapweed more than anything, but the bottoms of the draws had good grass. Even a slight curve or a small wall of earth obstructed the view, and twice in the morning Gene had spooked deer, which he did not see again. And so he followed the winding passages on Dodger, occasionally looking back and occasionally climbing up top to get his bearings.

When the sun was straight up, or close to it, and Gene was wondering when he might see the next cow, let alone a dry one, he heard the crash of a rifle shot, followed by a second one. Dodger stopped short and his ears came up. Gene listened. Nothing. His first thought was of Charlie Bickford, laying a stubbled jaw against the stock of a Winchester. He pulled his own saddle gun and pushed Dodger up the draw until he found a slope where they could climb up top. There was nothing in view, just the sparse ridges of the many-fingered drainages.

"Zeke!" he hollered, and the shout died away quickly. "Zeke!" Again nothing. He felt dry and dusty. Balancing his rifle across the saddle in front of him, he unslung his canteen and took a drink. The air was still and warm and dry.

Gene pushed Dodger back down into the draw and followed it back the way he had come, back toward the mouth. If Zeke was in trouble, it might take Gene all day to find him. A thickness welled up in his throat, and tears started in his eyes as he thought the words, *Zeke. My brother.*

At the mouth of the draw he made a hairpin turn and followed the path Zeke and Bucky had made in the grass. Twice the grass was flattened in both directions at a fork, and Gene let Dodger pick the way. Then he rounded a turn in the draw, and he saw something that chilled him. It was Zeke's hat, the high-crowned white hat, lying on its side on the trail.

Gene dismounted to pick up the hat and to look for what he hoped he wouldn't find — blood. But the grassy bottoms were poor for tracking the small details. He saw nothing.

He followed the draw for about as long as he had followed the first one, and still there was no sign of Zeke. Gene found a slope that would bring them up top, and when they got there he saw Zeke. His brother was still on Bucky, two ridges over and hatless with his right hand shading his eyes as he studied the country. They waved.

"I found your hat," Gene called out, as if that was all there was to it.

"Good," Zeke's one word simplified things right back.

"That wasn't you shooting, was it?"

"No."

"Well, it wasn't me."

"I know." Zeke scanned the country and with his rifle pointed to a spot where three fingers of

51

drainage came together. "Let's meet there," he said.

Then he dropped down into his gully, and Gene dropped into his, and they did not see each other again until the meeting spot.

"Thanks," Zeke said, as he received his hat.

"Did you get a look at who it was?"

"No, and to tell you the truth, I don't even know what direction the shots came from. The bullet slaps into the dirt, and then the sound comes walloping all around you, what with the way you are, down in these places."

"So you didn't see anyone."

"Not a thing. I figure whoever it was dropped down into another draw and slipped on out the back door."

Gene made wide eyes. "One good guess, eh?"

Zeke, whose good humor seemed to come trickling back, smiled and said, "Just one."

Gene and Zeke trailed twenty-two head back to the ranch on Wednesday evening. They made no mention of the shooting incident to the other hands, and without asking any direct questions they learned that Charlie had been riding line out south all week.

For the next three days they delivered salt with a team wagon, two men doing a one-man job. Gene wondered what Monte had figured for them, but he knew there was no point in asking.

Saturday night, during the poker game, Charlie was more even-tempered than he had been of late. As the punchers asked one another about conditions on the various ranges they'd been riding, Charlie asked and answered as much as anyone.

"How 'bout that country you and Gene went to?" he asked.

"Bad country for snakes," Zeke said, and the topic moved on.

On Sunday afternoon Gene cleaned up and shaved, put on a fresh shirt, checked the loads in his six-shooter, and put on his hat. "Well," he said to Happy, who had been briefed on the week's events, "I think I'll take a little ride out to Walter Rose's place."

"Sounds like a good idea. Be careful."

"Zeke's stayin' here. He'll know if anyone leaves behind me."

"I doubt that anyone will."

"I doubt it, too."

Gene cut across the country southeast, taking it at an easy lope in the warm sun. It was a wonderful country, he thought, all of it — the prairie, the broken country, the mountain. A man should feel free to be on easy terms with all of it, not have to worry if every rock or ridge hid a man with murder in his heart.

The carpet flowers were in bloom, and he knew the silk blossoms of prickly pear were not far away. For the next two months the prairie flowers would bloom in turn and the grass would be green. It was a good country year round, never easy, but this time of the year came close.

Katharine Rose was brushing her dun mare at the hitching rail when Gene rode into the yard.

She smiled and waved to him, set down her brush, and untied her horse, lest it spook at the stranger. Holding the lead rope with her left hand, she pushed her dark hair aside and shaded her eyes with her right. Her tanned face shone in the afternoon sun.

"Good afternoon, Gene."

"Afternoon," he said as he dismounted and faced her. He was struck again with the plain, simple beauty he saw in her. She was of average height and average build for a woman — nothing stunning, nothing out of the ordinary. But she was a vibrant person — he sensed it whenever he got near her. Now, as he looked at her tan face and saw the life in her eyes and the moisture in her half-open mouth, he thought of the phrase he had dwelled upon when he had seen her last: *as dark as cedar, as clear as well water.* Something inside him had thrilled at the first sight of her today, even from a distance. He didn't remember ever feeling the sensation with Ginny. Now with Katharine the feeling came on stronger than before, the clean cool thrill of being in the presence of a dynamic woman who had nothing to prove.

"What brings you here on a day like this?" she asked, smiling as if to say it was the right kind of day.

"Seemed like a nice day for a ride."

"You probably don't get to ride much," she teased.

"Not out this way."

"Where you been ridin' then, so far away?" She

pursed her lips in mock curiosity.

"Up north, off to the broken country. Makes me thirsty to think of it."

She laughed. "Well, come on over and sit in the shade, and I'll find us some cool water, and you can recover."

They led their horses to the shade of a cottonwood, where he held them both as she went into the house. She came out with a pitcher and two glass tumblers, and they sat on the ground with their knees nearly touching.

"Heard you had a little party last week," she teased.

"Henry must have filled you in."

"He mentioned it."

"I doubt he mentioned our guest of honor, unless he came by here again on the way home."

She gave him a curious look. "No."

"Charlie Bickford showed up, more or less invited himself."

"Life of the party, no doubt."

"Exactly. It was about as much fun as —"

"— indigestion."

Gene laughed. "That's it. He's a hard pill to swallow, all right."

"He comes by here to water his horse whenever he's within ten miles."

"I've gathered that."

"Thinks I ought to melt at the sight of him." She wrinkled her nose. "Doesn't quite happen."

"I guess he's been workin' down this way the last week."

"Just the last few days."

"Oh, really? I thought he came down here Monday."

"As far as I know, he wasn't around here till about Wednesday. I'd know, believe me."

"I believe you."

She looked at him closely. "Did you come down here to check up on him?"

"Not exactly. I'm not checkin' on him to report to anyone, but I am curious about where he was or wasn't, 'long about Monday or Tuesday."

"Oh," she said, which he interpreted to mean, "I won't ask any more."

Gene, who had ridden all this way with the firm intention of gathering information slyly and letting none out, felt as if a gate had just opened and he had stepped through it into a very pretty unfenced garden with Katharine Rose. It was safe, and no place to keep secrets. "Somebody took two shots at my brother Zeke when we were up north in the breaks. On Tuesday, when Charlie was supposed to be down this way."

Their eyes met. "Thank you," she said. "Thank you for feeling you could tell me that."

"One other thing," he said.

"What's that?" she asked, with concern still in her eyes.

"That's not the only reason I rode down here today."

"Yes . . ."

"I also came down here to see you, and to talk you out of a cool drink of water."

His right hand was lying on the ground, palm upward, and she reached her left hand so that her fingertips overlay his. "Thank you," she said, "for telling me that too."

CHAPTER 5

On the ride back to Redboot, Gene felt elated at having been in the company of Katharine Rose. Now, even more strongly than before, he felt that she might be the one to share the cabin a little farther down the trail.

When he thought of Ginny he envisioned her neat, blond hair, always washed and brushed, and her hands, neatly folded in her lap. Her clothes were always clean and pressed. Nothing was out of place — everything seemed to be in the right place. When he thought of her she was sitting in one place, and her life was surrounded by firm shapes — a stone fireplace, the walls of her parents' sitting room, the picket fence that enclosed the front yard.

When he thought of Katharine there weren't any enclosures. Life stretched out in all directions, across the rolling earth, from the wild roses and cedars and chokecherries she tended, to the prairie, canyons, and watercourses of the surrounding country where she found them. Life rippled outward from her with the sunshine and the breeze, and he felt a lightness of heart as he thought of her — the freedom he felt when he was riding the range with his brother Zeke or waking up on a cold clear morning in camp.

She seemed to Gene to be at ease in her world. She had a sure sense of herself. Her parents were not driving stakes in the ground for her. Walter Rose made a close living on a hardscrabble spread, running a few cattle and horses, and training draft horses for buggy and wagon work. He and his wife Emily were older as parents go, both of them in their sixties. Katharine, their only child, was a late advent in their lives. An occasional whisper had it that the child had been adopted as a baby, but that did not matter to Gene. He saw them as a family that lived together, close to the earth. They had brought her up that way, and it seemed they would let her live that way as she chose.

His mind traveled back to the image of Ginny in a lantern-lit room. It was all there, the things a man was supposed to reach for, if he could. He had been doing what he was supposed to do for quite a while. His sudden attraction to Katharine had caught him by surprise, but it seemed right. As Gene rode back to Redboot on this late Sunday afternoon, he knew he couldn't up and quit on Ginny just because things had taken a slowdown with her and a pickup with Katharine. No, he said to himself, it would take some seeing through.

Back at the bunkhouse, Gene had a quiet talk with Happy in the kitchen while the cook peeled potatoes. Happy was interested in Gene's account of his visit. He did not seem surprised to learn that Charlie hadn't been seen in the neighborhood until Wednesday, nor did he seem surprised that Charlie had been trying unsuccessfully to make a hit with Katharine.

"That explains one little incident while you were gone."

"Oh?"

"The boys were all talking the way they do, you know, small-talking about this and that, and someone mentioned where you had gone off to. Then Charlie passed a remark about a bitch in heat."

Gene's blood rose. "There's no end to his bad nature, is there? Anyone who knows her in the slightest would know better."

"Oh, shrug it off, Gene. It's just his cheap way of talk, you know that."

"Did anyone else say anything?"

"I did."

"What did you say?"

"I told him to clean it up, that no one wanted to hear that line of talk."

"What did he say to that?"

"He told me to mind my own business or he'd break these windows." Happy pointed at his eyeglasses, which had a few white specks from the potato peeling.

"Was Zeke there?"

"No, he was outside. But someone else — Jack, I think — told him to shut up, that he ought to know better than to pick on the cook."

"Well, good for Jack. But it just burns me up that he'd say something like that."

"Talk's cheap, Gene. You know that."

"Yeah, I know."

Sunday evening went without incident in the bunkhouse. Gene caught a look at Charlie from time to time and wondered what new shapes were forming out of the arrogance and hatred in the swaying head.

On Monday morning Monte had a genuine odd job for Gene and Zeke. There was a bull making trouble out on Feather Creek, due west from the ranch house and almost at the foot of the mountain. The bull, which had been known as Bad Oscar for years, had a reputation for being bad-tempered and unruly. He had always tried to hump the younger bulls, which was not unusual, but lately he seemed to have gotten worse, starting fights with other bulls. Now he had a broken prong, which didn't seem to have improved his disposition a bit.

"Bring him in if you can," Monte said. "He's worth a few dollars alive, the ornery old son of a bitch, so we'll try to do it that way. If he's too wild, then I guess you know what to do."

Gene and Zeke rode out of the yard as the sun was just coming up, spreading pink sunlight on the green grass and casting long, dancing shadows ahead of them. Gene felt the morning chill still on his shoulders.

"I'm not sure I know this Bad Oscar," Zeke said.

"He's a big brindle humpback, about a foot and a half between the eyes. He's been around for a while. He's got an old brand that's haired over and hard to read — but he's not original Redboot stock. He just moved in from somewhere else."

"Must've come in from Texas with the other riffraff," Zeke said grinning.

Gene laughed. "He's that kind, all right, long and rangy and probably tough as an old boot."

"Poor kind of beef cattle, really. They should've cut him for a steer when they had him down."

"Too late for that now."

"You said it. I'm not gettin' that close to him. He gets those stub horns too close, he could raise hell with Bucky and me both."

"We can handle him."

"Oh, yeah. Long rope and a little bit of luck, and we'll send his broken prick to Omaha."

They heard Bad Oscar half an hour before they reached him. He was standing on a knoll over the creek, alone, no other cattle in sight, bellowing at the creek bottom and slobbering on the ground he had pawed up. The brothers stopped at the bottom of the hill and looked at each other with a look that said, "Well, here it goes."

Their plan was for one of them to ride along on each side of Oscar and haze him along, if possible. If that didn't work, they would rope his horns from each side and make a slow balking drag back to the home corral. But if they could haze him a mile, even half a mile, it would be a lot of work saved.

Gene looked at the sky. It was barely past nine in the morning, and thunderheads were already building on the mountain. The chance of a sudden shower in this country was good at any time between April and October, and if it rained out on the open range, there was no way around it. Most frequently a storm just built up, poured down, and passed over, and a fellow didn't lose much work at all. But if this storm had thunder and lightning, it could make today's work memorable.

Zeke looked at the sky, too. "That's not goin' to help much."

Gene said, "Probably not. But I guess we'd just as well get started."

"I guess."

Both of them carried two ropes today, just for good measure. They each got a first rope ready, fingered the coils and shook out a loop, and side by side set out after Bad Oscar.

The first three minutes went fine. Zeke circled around in back of the bull and came up on the off side. Tossing the loop out and jerking the rope, he snapped the bull smart on the rump. Bad Oscar took off at a trot for the creek bottom, and Gene picked him up on the right side, keeping a safe distance. At the creek the bull turned left and followed the cow trail down through the brush and trees. Zeke followed on the left and Gene on the right, both of them skirting the growth along the bottom.

"Sooner or later we gotta get him up outa there," Zeke called. "We gotta get him up your side and out into the open."

"I know," Gene called back.

The bull, as if he had heard them, made a sharp left turn and came barreling up the bank directly across in front of Zeke. He was headed back to the knoll where they had started. Zeke circled around in back of him again while Gene came back across the creek. Twice more they hazed the bull to the creek, only to have him double around and void their efforts.

"We gotta get him across and up the other side," Zeke said. "Once we do that, we rope him, and I don't care if we have to drag him on his ass all the way back to the ranch."

"I've had enough of this, too," Gene agreed. "Let's get him."

They pushed him down into the creek again, Zeke staying a little wider this time. When the bull came out, Zeke was ready to head him off. Bucky, good cow pony that he was, figured out the game and played wolf-and-moose with the bull, cutting quickly to the right and left in short spurts and not letting the bull make progress. Finally the bull turned around and jogged back to the creek, and Zeke went pounding after it, shouting and slapping his loop on his boot. The bull charged on through and up the other side. Zeke followed as Gene rode up and turned out, so that the two of them sat facing the bull and had him blocked from coming back to the creek.

"We could try hazin' him," Gene said, "but we could fight this creek all day."

"We better rope him."

"Yeah."

Together they charged after Bad Oscar, who bolted, angling away to the right. Gene shook his loop as Dodger caught up, and then, smooth as spreading butter on a slice of bread, he slapped the loop over Oscar's stub horns and dallied his rope on the saddle horn. Oscar started fighting the rope, dragging Dodger and Gene along on halting lurches, as Zeke came up and dropped a second loop over the bull's horns. Just as the loop hit, the bull charged straight at Gene and Dodger, pulling the rope from Zeke's hand before he had a chance to dally. Dodger sidestepped and backed off, but Gene's rope went slack; then the bull was past them and whirled, hitting the end of the rope and bucking its full ton of fury. Gene, nearly jerked from the saddle, came up with his second rope but didn't have a plan for using it. Meanwhile Zeke had his second rope out, built his loop, and came around to rope Oscar's right heel.

The ground shook as the mad bull hit the ground, but the two horses held steady against the thrashing, and relative peace reigned for the moment. Gene looked at Zeke, who licked his lips and said, "Guess I'd better get that rope." He stepped off the right side of the saddle and walked cautiously to where the loose rope lay.

Gene watched, barely breathing. Had it been his rope, he would be doing the same thing, but it was Zeke's, so Gene got to stay in the saddle and admire his brother's cool courage.

Zeke took the loose rope and shook it once, twice, until the hondo loosened. Then he shook it again, and again, with the bull flailing all the time, until the loop grew and then flopped off the lethal horns. Zeke snapped the rope toward him and, backing off, coiled it up.

The bull settled and lay still. Gene let out his breath and looked at Zeke, who said, "Easy part's done. I think what we gotta do next is try to stagger him up the hill a ways, away from all this tangle, and get me a rope around his horns again. Then we can get this rope off his hock, dainty like, and waltz back to the ranch house."

Zeke walked around behind Bucky, patting him on the rump and all the time keeping an eye on the bull. Then, as he stepped into the left stirrup, all hell broke loose.

Bad Oscar lurched forward suddenly, jerking both horses forward at the same time and slackening the ropes before the horses could regain balance and tighten up. As the bull thrashed madly this way and that, it found new slack. Gene could feel Dodger fighting the renewed fury but losing his purchase on the sloping bank. He looked at Bucky, holding tight again but with an empty saddle, fighting backward as Zeke scrambled out of the way and to his feet.

Then Dodger gave way with a jerk, and Gene felt himself popped from the saddle. He landed on his left forearm and hip, painfully, but he lost no time rolling away, away from Bad Oscar fighting onto his front feet, away from Dodger thrashing and grunting, belly up and hooves pawing at the clouding sky.

"I'm gonna cut the rope!" Zeke yelled.

Gene came to his feet and saw Zeke grab the rope, the surging cable of power between the crazed bull and the kicking horse. Zeke's jackknife flashed in his right hand as, with his left arm taut and jerking with the jolts of the rope, he sawed and sliced through the rope strands.

Then the rope snapped apart, and it was every animal for himself. Zeke backed uphill as Dodger scrambled to his feet and galloped away clear. Gene moved back, sidehilling, as he watched the bull struggling to its feet and jerking Zeke's plucky cow horse like a fish on a line. Zeke ran and made a grab for the saddle, a more successful one this time, and Gene saw his intention: to give slack to the rope and free the dallies from the saddle horn.

But the timing was not quite right. Oscar was up and moving a split second too soon. Zeke put the spurs to Bucky, still working for slack but not getting it. Then Bad Oscar crashed into a wild plum thicket, dragging horse and rider sideways into the thorny tangle. The bull fell, still raging and thrashing, jerking his big fish an inch at a time. Gene knew there was only one way now, as he skirted the thicket and came up facing Oscar with the six-gun cocked and ready. The bull was not really a foot and a half between the eyes, and his head was flopping, but Gene managed to put a bullet there anyway.

Zeke got unhooked when the line went dead. He had his horse backed out free and was brushing him off when Gene came out to hand him his rope. Dust and the smell of the bull hung in the air. Gene was cotton-mouthed and was glad to see Zeke unslinging his canteen. Zeke took a long gurgling swallow and handed the canteen to his brother.

"That was a lousy sonofabitch of a job," he said.

Gene wiped his lips and nodded. "I didn't see any other way."

"Hell, no. We'd've been better off shootin' him when we first came up on him. If he could've been herded back, someone would've brought him in when he first started raisin' hell."

"We gave it an honest try."

"No doubt about that. I got no shame about how this one ended."

Then they heard horse hooves and looked around. It was Charlie Bickford coming down the slope, leading Dodger. Gene followed his glance as it found the brindle bull lying dead in the thicket. Charlie dropped Dodger's reins as he halted his horse and looked down at Zeke and Gene. His head swayed lightly, as it habitually did, and he smiled in evident satisfaction as he said, "Well, looks like you fellas ganged up on this one all right."

CHAPTER 6

Zeke stood with his back to Charlie as he tied the two ropes onto his saddle. Without looking at his nemesis he said, "Charlie, you're a ways off your range, ain't you?"

"This is Redboot range, and I work for Redboot."

"Why don't you work where you're sent?" Zeke turned to face him.

Charlie smirked. "I don't see what that matters to you. Why don't you do a job right when you're sent?"

Zeke didn't answer. He just spit on the ground.

Charlie's face seemed to glow with satisfaction as it bobbed. The bruise from the last fight was gone, but not the gloating confidence that he was the better man. Then Gene saw that in his right hand, on the off side of his horse, Charlie had the half rope that had been dallied to Dodger's saddle. Gene knew it was his rope because he saw the frayed end sticking out at the top of the coils.

Then Zeke spoke. "When I get sent out I do my work whether I botch it or not, but I go where I'm sent and do what I'm told."

"I can't help it if I hear a shot and see a horse

runnin' loose. I thought maybe little brother here had fell off his horse and shot hisself in the foot."

"Seems like you might be handy at bein' close at hand when there's shots to be heard."

"What do you mean by that?"

"Last Tuesday," Gene cut in.

"You just keep out of this, little brother," Charlie said, turning to Gene and pointing with the hand that held the rope. Gene saw that the rope hung in three or four long loops. "You already done your teamwork for the day," he went on. "Why don't you take a rest and keep out of this."

"How about last Tuesday?" Zeke asked.

"How 'bout it?" Charlie spit off to the right.

"Someone took two shots at me up in the breaks."

"And you think it was me."

"I think it was somebody who was where he wasn't supposed to be."

"Did he miss?"

"What do you think?"

"Must not have been me. Let me tell you two things, Zeke Hill. When I shoot to hit, I don't miss. And I don't need a rifle to take care of you."

Zeke stung him. "You gonna do it with words?"

Charlie swung the loose rope and knocked Zeke's hat off, then tossed the rope aside as he stepped out of the saddle. He looked large and terrible as he stood uphill from Zeke, all of his suppressed rage having come to the surface. He was about three inches taller than Zeke and a good thirty pounds heavier, but he was in good condition and moved smoothly, setting his hat on the saddle horn and sending his horse out of the way, all the while keeping his eye on the man he hated.

Zeke, having dodged the swipe that knocked off his hat, was straightened back up and ready for Charlie. But this time he was not prancing around and fighting for fun. Gene could see Zeke was concentrating, ready for the worst and determined to win.

Gene looked at Charlie. If the man had a weakness, it was his confidence he would come out on top, the assurance that when he was done he would walk right back to his horse, put his hat back on his head, and ride away.

Gene looked back at Zeke, black hair matted down and the widow's peak pointing into his brow. Zeke's eyes glared, and the firmness of his jaw showed that the teeth were clenched. Gene knew his brother. Zeke felt he could win but he wasn't sure he would. That could save him.

Charlie moved in quickly, faking two left jabs and connecting with a glancing right cross. Zeke took the punch moving to the right, and as he did so he counterpunched Charlie, rocking the red head and stopping the man's forward motion.

Zeke skipped out backward, regrouped, and came back in, feinting. He and Charlie traded about four punches each, and then they backed off for an instant. It was still an even, standup fight, but not for long. Charlie rushed at his man, head just slightly lowered so that Gene could see the balding spot.

Zeke caught him with a cowcatcher, and for a moment the two of them grappled to see who could get the other in a bear hug, to smash him to the ground. Neither of them succeeded at getting the grip. Then Zeke put both hands around Charlie's skull with his fingertips touching and almost locking in back. He flung the head forcefully downward and moved aside, and as Charlie stumbled forward, Zeke tackled him.

The fight became terrible; Gene could feel the raw power in the air. The two bodies rolled and snarled, entangled so that Gene could not tell whose limbs were whose. Both men seemed to be consumed by an animal hatred. Gene felt a steady current of fear within, fear of what Zeke might do to Charlie. Gene knew he had to stay out of it, but he also knew that if Charlie got the upper hand and took it too far, he would have to do something to save his brother.

Charlie was on his back now; Zeke had a left hand on his throat and was smashing him in the face with his right. Zeke had his own head pulled back, to lessen the impact of Charlie's flailing right hand. Zeke's face seemed to show pain, sick pain, and then Gene saw why. Charlie's left hand was on Zeke's crotch. Their animal oneness now separated: there was a black-headed man and a red-headed one.

All of a sudden Charlie heaved and bucked, releasing his grasp on Zeke and wrenching the left hand from his throat. The men rolled for a turn and a half, and Charlie came up clenching Zeke's head in a left-arm headlock. Zeke reached up with his right hand and got a fistful of Charlie's thinning red hair and yanked the head back.

Then Charlie did something that made Gene sicken. Cupping his left hand on Zeke's chin to hold the headlock, he settled his right hand across Zeke's nose and mouth and began to work his thumb into Zeke's eye socket.

Zeke went wild, all the way this time. He yanked Charlie's head back savagely and, sweeping with his left arm, rolled Charlie over him and onto his back. Zeke drove his knee into the pit of Charlie's stomach, which seemed to knock most of the fight out of him. Then, straddling the man who had tried to gouge out his eye, Zeke settled both hands on his throat and slammed his head into the ground, again and again and again, even after the man beneath him had quit writhing and kicking.

Gene heard himself shouting. "Zeke! That's enough! He's finished! Zeke! Let go! You'll kill him!"

Then Zeke did let go, and the head sank to the ground and lolled to one side and was still. Zeke stared, clearly startled, then crawled off of the man. Still on all fours, he moved a few yards away, where he shifted into a sitting position.

Gene came and squatted by him. "Are you all right?"

Zeke nodded, trembling. "Yeah, I'm all right. I don't know if I killed him."

They both looked at the sprawled body. There was not a trace of motion. "Let's just sit here a little while," Gene said. "You can get yourself to-gether, and we'll see if he comes around."

Zeke nodded and swallowed.

"You want a drink of water, Zeke?"

"Yeah," he said, heaving. "I could sure use one."

Gene brought the canteen they had drunk from earlier. Zeke took it with shaking hands and said, "Thanks, Gene."

Gene squatted again. He patted his brother on the shoulder and said, "Just get yourself together. We'll just sit here and keep an eye on him."

Zeke took out the makings, but his hands were too shaky to roll a cigarette. Gene rolled it for him and let him lick it; then he tapped it and smoothed it and stuck it in Zeke's mouth. Zeke grinned and said, "Thanks." He lit his cigarette himself, took a short drag and then a long one, exhaled heavily, and said, "Something happened when I felt him try to gouge out my eye."

"I saw him do it."

"It was like everything was even up until then, but when he tried that, something snapped inside of me and I couldn't stop."

"I doubt he would've stopped any sooner on you."

"No, I doubt it, too. I guess I'm the lucky one."

A few drops of rain began to patter. "Damn," Gene said. "It looks like it's goin' to rain. I'd better gather up the horses. You stay here and finish your smoke."

Zeke exhaled through his nose, nodded, and said, "Okay."

When Gene got back with the horses he asked, "Has he moved?"

"Not a bit."

Gene walked softly over to the body. With the toe of his boot he nudged a leg. It rolled back into place. He pushed at the rib cage. Again no reaction. Sidestepping the outflung arm, he toed the head, which also sank back to rest. The eyelids were closed, and raindrops had fallen on them. "I think he's done for, Zeke." Gene knelt and felt the man's wrist and neck, but there was no pulse. "Yeah. I think so, Zeke."

Zeke was shaking his head and picking at the grass where he sat. "I didn't have any intention of killing him. But then again, I guess I wasn't trying not to."

"Well, it's done. What do we do now? Load him up and haul him in?"

Zeke's humor seemed to be on the way back. "Yeah, we could ride into the yard and say, 'Well, Gene killed Oscar, and I killed Charlie. Didn't mean to, but we got 'er done by noon.' "

Gene laughed, the nervous laugh of dread that still felt good. "What do you think, then?"

"I don't know. We ought to have time to haul Charlie out to the south range where he was supposed to be, and let his horse go in from there."

"Then we come back this way and go home?"

"What do you think?"

"I guess it'll look like his horse spooked in the storm and threw him." Gene grimaced. "There's no bullet holes or knife marks in him."

"I doubt it could ever come back on us, especially in this rain."

Gene nodded slowly. Everyone knew there was bad blood between Zeke and Charlie, and there was no guarantee they would take Zeke and Gene's word for how the fight had gone. Zeke's plan seemed like the easy way, the line of least resistance. If it looked like Charlie died out on his own range, there wouldn't be many questions raised.

Charlie's horse was not cooperative, so they had to blindfold him with a jacket and tie his front left foot up off the ground. Then they wrestled and heaved Charlie up and across the saddle, and tied him tight.

By now the rain was soft and steady, a misty rain in low clouds, which would keep visibility down to short distances. That would mean less chance of being seen, but less chance also of seeing someone else.

Gene's stomach was all in a knot as they set out leading their dead freight. Charlie's horse settled down once it got out on the trail with the other two, and Gene kept them all at a brisk walk. Zeke seemed to be sitting painfully in the saddle, and when Gene asked him if he was all right, he said, "Sonofabitch got his hand on me pretty good. But I'll be all right. Better'n I can say for him."

All the way to the south range, which measured about fifteen miles the long way around, Gene had the overwhelming sense of a bad thing that couldn't be undone. Occasionally he looked back, not that he needed reminding, but to check to see that the burden was riding even on its horse.

They left Charlie face up on an alkali flat, sprawled out as he had been when Zeke crawled off him. They tossed his hat on the ground nearby. Rain began to speckle the front of his clothes, which had been underside and had remained mostly dry on the trip over. Gene looked at the face, which seemed to have lost its gloating expression, and he realized the swaying head had come to a rest at last.

Turning Charlie's horse loose, they rump-slapped it in the direction of headquarters. Then they headed back toward Feather Creek, covering ground faster now than before, even though Zeke was clearly hurting.

As they rode, Gene's mind returned again and again to the image of an upturned face with water beading on it and running down the grizzled cheeks. He had wanted to form the words "I'm sorry, Charlie," but they hadn't come strongly enough, and he hadn't been able to make himself say something he only halfway felt.

All the same, there was a man dead on the cold plains back there, and it couldn't ride lightly with a man — not with Gene, certainly, and not with his brother, regardless of how Zeke might put on a show of having brushed it all off.

The man was dead, killed by another man. Whether it was justified or not, it couldn't be denied. Gene shook his head. It was pointless, a needless waste of a life. If Charlie had not become such a hard man in a hard world, it would not have come to this.

A man was dead and for not very good reasons. Maybe Charlie had been, as Jack Townsend had said, a real piss-pot lately if not always. But he was somebody's son and somebody's brother, and that made him someone to be mourned.

Gene looked at his own brother, still alive and riding tough. He couldn't blame Zeke for the outcome. Charlie had tried to kill him more than once; Gene was sure of that.

When they got back to Feather Creek, the rain was still falling soft and steady. Gene could not pick out their own tracks from earlier. That was good.

He drew up at the place where everything had gone wrong.

"What do you want to stop here for?" Zeke asked.

"Wait up here for a minute. I want to go down and get the other half of my rope from around Bad Oscar's horns."

CHAPTER 7

The death of Charlie Bickford was a matter of greater concern than the death of Bad Oscar, but neither event made much of a change in the daily goings-on at Redboot.

There wasn't a great deal made of Charlie's death. His horse had come in with an empty saddle and no blood on it, just before sundown. The next morning broke clear and sunny, and Pete Bonair and Rusty George went out to look for Charlie. They found him, of course, and came back for a wagon. That afternoon Monte drove the wagon to town and sent a message up Kaycee way, where Chet Bickford was holding down a job. Chet sent word that the body should be freighted to Casper, a two-day haul, where he would arrange for burial. In the same telegram he mentioned that he would be around later to pick up Charlie's gear. And so Charlie was gone, without ceremony or even much talk.

As cowhands knew, it could happen to any of them — death on the open range, far from family, home, or friends. They had all been on hand to bury men they liked much better than Charlie, and it had become their common way to accept the unchangeable and say little about it. Yet Gene imagined that each of the hands gave much more thought to Charlie's passing than he let on outwardly.

To Gene's way of thinking, there should have been a little more stir about Charlie's going. Undoubtedly, what little there was had been minimized by the enormity of the event in Gene's mind, but even as he considered that idea, he thought there should have been a little more said, a little more of a shake-up in the life of the ranch.

Monte might have chosen to split up Gene and Zeke, but for his own reasons he chose not to. Instead he hired a young cowhand who went by the name of Tommy Tipton. Tommy was an alert, go-ahead sort of a young man that bosses liked. He was also good-natured and polite, a welcome change from his predecessor. He was originally from Ohio, that part of Ohio where the folks talked like Kentuckians. Tommy was all of nineteen, but two years in the Nebraska sandhills had made him an able cowpuncher.

Gene was troubled at having to hide the truth from Happy. Once, in a conversation with Tommy and Happy, Gene said it was too bad a man died just like that and it didn't seem to change anything.

"Not a plow stops when a man dies," said Happy, which had the effect that proverbs often do, of closing rather than opening a topic.

On another occasion, when it was just the two of them, Gene said, "I wonder when Chet will come by."

Happy set down the book he had been reading, *The Portrait of a Lady*, and said, "That's an interesting speculation."

"Oh, no," Gene said quickly. "I just wish he was here and gone, that's all."

"He'll be here soon enough, I suppose," Happy said, and he took up his book again.

Up until now, Gene had always been able to discuss things openly with his friend. Now it seemed as if there was an uneasiness on each side.

With Zeke too, there seemed to have developed an invisible barrier. He and Gene still worked together, day by day, and yet they never mentioned the fight on Feather Creek. Zeke's good-natured, luck-is-with-me attitude shone through as clearly as ever. Zeke whistled as he dug postholes, showed off his waltz step as he balanced a shovel upright on his finger tip. Outside the bunkhouse he lagged pennies with the other men; inside, he would cut the deck for high card, a penny per cut. He seemed as carefree as the day he'd come back from Texas, and maybe he was.

It was during the first two weeks after Charlie's death, as Gene wrestled with his own conscience, that he paid a visit to Virginia Bransford. He did not yearn to see her, but he felt he had to follow through in his courtship. And so he ended up, once again, hat in hand, in the Bransford sitting room, seeing the bright clean woman, smelling her perfume over the background aroma of kerosene, and sensing the glow of past flames in the solid stone fireplace.

On the day of the picnic he had felt as if she saw him as an average, well-meaning cowpoke who associated with the less-desirable likes of Zeke and Charlie. This evening he was comforted even less, imagining what she would think of him if she knew the truth — that he had stood by while his brother killed a man with his bare hands and that he, Eugene Hill, had helped cover up the deed. He wondered if, having done what he had done, he could even think of marrying her. And if by some stretch he should marry her, could he ever, ever tell her? He probably could not, but he would have one loophole: In the world she lived in, there were some things a man never told a woman.

This evening the talk was not of murder or hideous guilt, but of life and its prospects. If a young man was courting a young woman, it seemed, the question had to come up: What would you like life to consist of, if you could have things go the way you'd like them to? She had asked the question as if it were a dreamy, romantic piece of philosophical speculation, and Gene appreciated the dressing she gave it. But in reality it was a necessary, practical topic, and he answered without much embellishment.

"I don't think I could be content working for a cowhand's wages the rest of my life."

Smiling, she nodded her encouragement to speak on.

"Some fellas, like Rusty George, don't seem to have much drive to do more than that. Others, like Jack Townsend, they probably have their sights fixed on a foreman's job at some big outfit. I see myself as working long enough to get together a stake, takin' up a place of my own, runnin' my own stock — bein' independent."

"A rancher, then."

"I guess so. I guess if you make a go of it, they'll call you a rancher sooner or later."

"You have a modest way of describing an admirable ambition, Gene. You sound like you know what you want."

"I've been workin' for wages for quite a few years now, and I've had time to think it over."

"I'm sure it's not just a general idea and nothing more. I'm sure you've got ideas about how all the little steps are done."

Gene felt as if he were being invited to expand on his strategy for selecting a homestead site, picking out good breeding stock, and building a herd — all of which, like any other cowpuncher who built air castles on horseback, he had thought about in extensive detail. "There's a whole system to be worked out," he began.

"I'm sure you'll do really well at it," she said.

He turned the topic back to her. "And yourself? How about you? I've often wondered what a town girl thinks of what this country has to offer."

"Well, for a town girl," she said, "I suppose I'm pretty typical. I've seen a little of the world, and I'd like to see more. But of course I know I can't determine the details of where I'll live and what I'll see."

"You have some choice," he said.

"That's true. A woman tries to do well for herself. But she can't control her husband's affairs and fortunes." She smiled openly at him. "I'm being horribly frank with you. I think you bring it out in me."

"I appreciate it," he answered. "You have a good idea of what you want or expect out of life, and I have a good idea of what I hope for. And we're interested in finding out about one another."

"You're chivalrous, Gene."

"In what way?"

"Other men would be trying to get me to say I welcomed the opportunity to milk cows, feed chickens, and plant spuds."

"That's not all there would be to it."

"Oh, I know. I was trying to be humorous."

"I think I followed that," he said, laughing.

"Thank you," she said, laughing back. "Sometimes it's hard to be funny."

"But you're not all that stuck on it, all the same — plantin' spuds and all."

"There are a lot of worse possibilities."

"But there are better ones, too."

"As possibilities go, yes, there probably are."

From there the talk trailed away into more general and pleasant topics, mainly of her devising: how wonderful it was that life lay wide open; how blessed they were to live in a civilized, prosperous country; how gratifying it was to know that there were some people with whom one could be always honest.

When Gene left that evening he did not take

her hand, much less try to kiss her.

"Thank you for coming," she said.

"Thank you for the conversation."

"I enjoyed it."

Gene let out a deep breath as he untied his horse and tightened the cinch. Yes, there could be worse possibilities. He could still be pursuing a dead-end courtship. At least he knew there was no future for Ginny and him. He was grateful she had not made him feel foolish for having courted her this long.

On the way home, one thought rankled him more than once. It was her comment about honesty. She had meant it, and he had wished he deserved it. It bothered him more than once on the way home, and it bothered him the most when he rode through a dry wash and then slowed the horse so he could pick out a ribbon of wagon track threading south in the moonlight.

Knowing that it was over with Virginia took a small weight off Gene's mind — small in comparison with the business about Charlie, but appreciable all the same. With respect to women, at least, the trail of life did not have a fork in it anymore. His affection was no longer divided. His mind was set on Katharine, although he knew he couldn't make any assumptions about her, either.

On his next visit to Katharine, the wild roses were blooming. As he got closer to her place he kept his eye out, and on the cutbank of a small gully he found a patch of the pink flowers. He cut a sprig that had three buds, then lost no time in getting to her yard.

She was standing in front of the weathered barn, hand-feeding grain to a fawn antelope, when he rode up. At the sight of the stranger, the antelope wheeled and dashed away. Katharine turned and waved at her visitor and came walking toward him. Again he was moved by the clear, strong beauty of the dark-haired woman in a plain cotton shirt and trousers. He dismounted and offered the sprig of rosebuds to her.

"How nice! Why, thank you, Gene." She fixed them into her hair, over her left ear. "June," she said, "the month of the wild rose." Then, at Gene's questioning look, she added, "That's in the Indian way of measuring time. They have their own calendar, of course."

"Right. They even have one for the wild plums ripening, don't they?"

"Yes, I think that one is August." She took a second just to smile at him, then said, "Come see mine. They're blooming, too."

She led him to the south side of the ranch house, where on his last visit she had shown him the bed of wild roses. The bed was about two feet wide and ran nearly the full width of the board house, perhaps twenty feet. The roses had just leafed out when he had seen them before, but today, swaying in the light breeze, they were in full color, with scarlet buds that had not yet opened and pink blooms that had. The little bushes did not have thick foliage, and the flowers were not profuse.

The distribution seemed to be in harmony with the setting.

"Whew!" he said, struck by the spareness and the richness of the scene. "That's something." Then he looked at the sprig in her hair. "I feel foolish bringing you that little snip."

She laid her left hand against the buds, as if to assure their security. "These are special," she said. "Special because they come from their natural home, and because you brought them." She half-grimaced. "Sometimes I almost feel guilty about these," she said, indicating her transplants with a sweep of her right hand. "I took them from their home and put them here. But," she added quickly, "they have an easier life here, and they're still wild."

Gene smiled and nodded. "It would seem to me that wherever you dug these up, there would be more growing back in their place, the way the roots grow."

"You're right. I've gone back to check, and they do."

Gene heard the *tinkle-tweet* of a meadowlark. "Oh, by the way, I'm sorry I spooked off your little friend. The antelope."

"Oh, him. Isn't he the cutest little orphan? He's been around for about two weeks now. But it's just as well he doesn't get too comfortable around humans anyway."

"Probably live longer," he said casually. Then he realized he had made a small blunder. Walter Rose's family was known to eat antelope, which was common fare on their spread. People who were situated more advantageously could have their pick of stray unbranded beef, deer, or maybe even elk — all of which most people preferred over antelope. But Walter, as Gene knew him, was content to take what came his way.

"Oh, Daddy wouldn't hurt him. And besides, there are lots more out there."

"I guess I was thinking of men in general. These antelope move around quite a bit, come and go."

She nodded, and then, as if a cloud had passed over, she said, "I hadn't thought of that. Men like — I'm sorry, I know it's not right to speak ill of the dead, but — men like Charlie Bickford. He used to shoot them just for target practice. That could be what happened to this one's mother, for all I know."

"He used to brag he could hit one on a full run at two hundred yards. That's not an easy thing to do."

"Well, I think he had plenty of practice." Then, as if to brighten the subject, she said, "That new boy they have, Tommy Tipton, seems nice."

"Does he water his horse here, too?"

"Oh, Gene, he's just a boy." She laid her hand on his forearm as her eyes met his. Then she cast her head downward in a mock pout, still looking up at him through her dark eyelashes. "Are we just a little bit jealous?"

He moved his arm so that her hand slipped into his. "I think I'm getting over it pretty quick." Then he added, "Did he tell you anything about me?"

"Like what?"

"Did he tell you I wasn't seeing Henry Bransford's sister anymore?"

They began walking around to the north side now, toward the shade tree. "He said something like that."

"How did you get that out of him?"

"It wasn't too hard. He's just a boy." Her eyes twinkled, then softened as she paused and turned to look at him. "I'm sorry if there was a falling off of friendship there, Gene."

"There wasn't, really. I'd say she and I are still friends. There's just been a cooling off, not that things were that simmering before."

"I would hope it hasn't hurt you, you know."

"No, I think it made things easier."

"I hope it turns out for the best. I could tell something was bothering you."

"Talking about it made it better. But it hasn't been bothering me all that much."

They were walking again as she said to him, sideways, "Is there some other thing bothering you?"

He could not lie to her. "Yes, there is."

"Is it anything you can talk about with me?"

He felt the gate open, and beyond it he saw the natural, unbordered garden. It was green, and it sparkled with the small, mixed blooms of wildflowers. Then the gate closed. "Not really," he said. "There's been some trouble, but I don't want to burden you with it."

89

"It wouldn't be a burden."

He laughed, nervously. "If you knew about it, it would be. I'm sorry — I don't mean to sound mysterious."

"It's all right," she said. "I asked."

"Well, that's the best answer I can give you right now."

"Gene?"

"Yes?"

"If the time does come when you feel right about telling me, will you, even if it's bad?"

The gate swung open and closed again. "Even if it's bad."

"Promise?" She pressed her hand on his chest, lightly.

"I promise."

Then their lips met for the first time, not for long, as they stood in the afternoon shade of the cottonwood tree, with the unpainted ranch house in the background.

When Gene rode home a little later, he remembered her as he saw her when he opened his eyes after the first kiss — dark as cedar, clear as well water, with a sprig of wild roses in her hair. Then he realized that wild roses didn't have much of a scent, not even a whole bed of them. He thought hard. Had there been a scent to Katharine? Yes, there had — the smell of sun and prairie breeze on clear skin and dark hair.

As he rode, he also debated with himself about the burden of secrecy. Should he have told her more? Did he let slip too much as it was? He felt confident that, for the present, it was better not to tell her. It would make her an accomplice, in a way, giving her a part in a bad thing that was not of her making. He hoped that as time passed and he saw matters more clearly, saw how Charlie's death was absorbed into the broader order of things, he would be able to lighten his burden by sharing it with her.

But the gate was closed now, the gate that led into the garden of open confidence. Worse, it was not closed by a sudden gust of wind but partly by his own hand — and partly by the hand of his brother Zeke.

CHAPTER 8

Gene had a peculiar dream that night, peculiar in
several respects. For one, Happy had a girlfriend,
a brown-haired widow lady, somewhere between
thirty-five and forty. She lived in a whitewashed
clapboard house all by itself on the prairie. Gene
could remember knowing all this about her, even
though he never saw her in the events of the dream.
Another oddity was that Gene and Happy went
on a lark like a couple of schoolboys, deciding to
pay Happy's girlfriend a surprise visit. As they
sneaked across the open prairie toward a side window in the little house, they saw Zeke's buckskin
tied to the hitching rail around the corner in front.
Then, from beneath the open window, Gene and
Happy heard a rhythmic creaking, thrashing sound
that could mean only one thing. Along with the
sounds of motion came the cooing, moaning voice
of a woman: "Oh, Zeke. Oooh. Zeke. You're so
good, Zeke." Gene remembered looking at Happy
and feeling sorry for him while hating his brother.

In the cold sober light of day, Gene thought
it over as he worked with Zeke and took frequent
looks at him. They were working on Monte's second holding pen, which they had been working

on since the failed mission to bring in Bad Oscar. Gene had been aware of a separation between himself and Zeke since the day of the picnic, and now he felt it even more keenly. Zeke, of course, had not committed the treachery as Gene had played it out in his own dream, but Gene felt that the dream reflected the widening of distance between him and his brother.

Around the bunkhouse, whenever a fellow talked about an unusual dream he had, someone usually had the comment, "Them dreams are just in yer head, y'know." That joke had always seemed to Gene to be a sort of whistling in the dark, pretending to deny the obvious truth that dreams came from somewhere and probably meant something.

What this dream meant exactly was, of course, impossible to know. But Gene imagined that at the bottom of it was his own regret for the closing off of confidence between himself and Happy, and between himself and Katharine. The barriers had arisen as a result of his having done things Zeke's way. He imagined that in his dream he was blaming Zeke, exaggerating Zeke's action into treacherous, headstrong selfishness.

He continued to study his brother as they dug their separate postholes, sweating under the June sun. It was not all Zeke's fault. He, Gene, the man on the end of this shovel, had acted in free will in covering up an act that would look much worse having been covered up. It was his mistake as well as Zeke's. He could not undo or redo what had happened that day. The trail of life ran one way.

At midday, as they ate cold beef and biscuits, Gene brought up the subject. Neither of them had spoken of it since it happened, but he saw no reason why he couldn't talk about the incident with the one other person who knew.

He said, "I suppose you've done some thinkin' about the way things went with the business about Charlie."

"You mean the way we did things."

"Yeah."

"Well, sure, I've thought about it."

"Do you wish we had done things different?"

"Not really."

"I guess I do."

Zeke chewed for a little while before answering. "I can't blame you. You never know if some of it will come back on you. Right now it doesn't seem like it. We seem to be in the clear. But you never know."

Zeke seemed unaffected by the kind of guilt that Gene felt weighing so heavily on himself. Gene looked past him to the mountain, where a layer of gray clouds was beginning to build. "I just don't like having to be so guarded," he said.

"I don't either," Zeke answered, "but I have more of a stake in it. That's what makes us different on this."

"I suppose so."

"I never killed a man before, Gene."

"I didn't think you had."

"Next to that, pretendin' that I didn't is a pretty small thing."

"I can see that . . . but it's the whole thing to me, the death, and then coverin' it up."

"Well, Charlie's dyin' was a bad thing to happen, but I can't regret protectin' myself."

"I can go along with that."

"Well, it just goes around in a circle. Coverin' it up is small potatoes compared to killin' him, which itself is somethin' I just accept. It happened. And I've been lucky not to be found out." Zeke shook his head as he chewed off a chunk of cold beef. "I just can't let myself get too worked up over somethin' I can't change."

"From this point in time, you're right. But we didn't have to do things that way at the time."

"It all seemed to flow together at the time."

"That it did," Gene conceded.

"And it can't be changed."

"No, it can't be changed."

After that, Gene did not bring up the subject again with Zeke. He could see that Zeke had a larger stake in the business and fewer scruples about how it had been handled. Gene also saw that among the things that couldn't be changed was Zeke's attitude on the whole affair.

Although Zeke's nonchalance was irritating, Gene thought that maybe his brother was better off not worrying until there was something to worry about. When someone asked Zeke how he won so many hands at poker, Zeke's favorite answer, whether he had been holding cards or bluffing, was "Just lucky, I guess." Maybe he was lucky here too, Gene thought, in having less of a conscience about what had happened with Charlie.

Zeke's good luck and light conscience both came into view in Saturday's poker game. With Tommy Tipton the game was five-handed again, and Gene sat on the outskirts with Happy as the latter smoked his pipe. Gene didn't mind sitting in on the game to fill out a hand at the table, but he didn't have a great flair for the game and preferred to be left out.

They were playing dealer's choice, and Zeke was having a good night. He was doing especially well at his own game, a seven-card stud game that he called every time the deal came around to him. "We'll play seven-card stud, one-eyed cowboy wild," he would say, as if it were the first time he had called it.

Once, Jack Townsend spoke up. "Why call 'em cowboys?"

Zeke replied in a mimicking tone, "Some folks calls 'em kings, some folks calls 'em cowboys."

Gene imagined that Zeke was imitating a voice from some other poker table in the past.

"What's wrong with callin' 'em like anyone else would?" Jack returned.

"I calls 'em cowboys," Zeke continued. "What's wrong with that?"

"There's other people that call 'em that too," said Rusty George.

"You want I should call 'em cowpunchers?" Zeke persisted, in the borrowed voice.

"Call 'em what you want," Jack conceded. "A cowpuncher's a cowboy. A cowpuncher's a king. A king's a cowboy. Call 'em what you want."

"I calls 'em cowboys," Zeke rippled, as he dealt the cards with an exaggerated flourish.

And so the table talk went on, until the subject came around to Charlie Bickford. Gene and Happy both paid attention.

"Poor way to die," Zeke said.

"Lotsa men die that way," Jack Townsend put in.

"That don't mean it's good," Zeke replied. They were playing five-card draw, open on guts, and the first round of betting was over. "I'll take three," he said, flipping his discards in the middle and picking up his new cards.

"No one said it was good," Rusty answered. "Least of all Pete and me. We found him."

"I'll take one," Jack Townsend said.

"Here's one," said Pete, who was at Zeke's right and dealing this hand.

"I'm out," said Tommy Tipton.

"I'll take two," said Rusty George. Gene saw him look knowingly at Pete as the cards were dealt.

"Dealer takes one," Pete said, discarding and then slapping down a new card for himself. "This one." Pete studied his cards. "Of course it wasn't good. Your bet, Zeke."

"Blue chip. Y'know, it's almost as if folks are afraid to talk about Charlie."

You've got a hell of a lot of nerve, Zeke, Gene thought to himself.

"Call your blue chip," Jack said.

Tommy pushed his chair back. "I'm already out."

"Call," said Rusty George. "What's there to be afraid of? The man's dead. But some things just don't look right."

"I fold," Pete Bonair said.

"What didn't look right?" asked Tommy Tipton, who suddenly looked uncomfortable at the thought of riding a dead man's range.

"For one thing," Rusty said, "it was rainin'."

"What's wrong with that?" Zeke interrupted.

"Let me talk, will ya? It was rainin'. But Charlie wasn't wearin' a jacket. His slicker was still tied on his saddle."

Pete was collecting the discards and folded hands. "If the horse threw him because of the storm — crash of thunder, bolt of lightnin', or whatever — then the storm had already started, and he should've been wearin' his jacket."

"Point two," Rusty George went on. "It wasn't that fierce a storm. It didn't blow up and thunder 'n' lightnin' like hell. It came on sudden-like, but it was a slow, steady rain, leastwise it was everywhere else."

"It was, out on Feather Creek," Zeke added, "where Gene and I were. But that's a good twelve miles away. What was it like down that way?"

"Nobody knows," Rusty said.

"For all that it matters," Jack Townsend said, "Walter Rose would know."

"All right," resumed Rusty George, who seemed to Gene to be either enjoying the role of detective or delaying the game for a tactical advantage. "So maybe it was stormin' like hell, maybe it wasn't. Maybe he should've been wearin' a jacket by then. Maybe his horse threw him for no reason."

"It does sound a little out of line," Zeke conceded, looking at his cards.

"Then figger this," Rusty went on. "The back of his shirt was wet."

"That would make sense if he wasn't wearin' a jacket," Zeke said.

Shut up, Zeke, Gene thought. Please shut up.

Happy spoke up. "I see what Rusty means. There are too many contradictions."

"And the ground was wet underneath him," Rusty threw in, as Happy puffed on his pipe.

"That goes along with his shirt being wet," Happy continued. "And that raises the question. Or questions. How bad was the storm? Why did the horse throw him, if that is what happened — as it seems to be? And why did he ride so long without a jacket or slicker? And if he did, wouldn't the ground have been soft? By the way, does anyone know for sure that he died from a blow to the head? Men have been known to keel out of the saddle with a heart attack or stroke, even in the full flush of health like Charlie."

"The back of his head was soft," Pete said, with evident reluctance. "Sort of pulpy."

"It reminds me of a similar thing that happened to me," Zeke began.

For heaven's sake, shut up, Zeke, Gene wanted to scream.

But Zeke went on, rolling a cigarette as he told the story, with his poker hand lying on the table with a blue chip on top of it. "Happened not too far from there, for that matter, about four years ago. I was ridin' along on Bucky, and the next thing I knew, the lights went out. I come to, I don't know how much later, with my left foot caught in the stirrup and me draggin' on the ground. Bucky was just nibblin' grass, and every time he stepped forward, the back of my head would go clunk on the ground. I think that's what woke me up — that, and there was a little rain fallin' at the time, too." Zeke lit his cigarette.

"Was the back of your shirt wet, too?" Jack asked, straight-faced.

"No, but I'd pissed my pants."

The bunkhouse exploded with laughter.

"Anyway," said Happy, relighting his pipe, "there are still some questions unanswered, hovering in the air, you might say."

"Does anybody know?" asked Jack Townsend. "Or, for that matter, does anybody care?"

"Too bad his horse can't talk," Rusty George said, seeming anxious to resume a lead role in the discussion.

"Maybe a good thing for somebody," quipped Pete Bonair.

"Why is that?" inquired Happy.

"Charlie had a bruise on his throat," Rusty George stated almost triumphantly.

Happy raised his eyebrows and blew out a cloud of smoke. "That might be of interest to somebody."

"His brother Chet, for example," Jack Townsend said with evident displeasure.

After a split second of silence Pete Bonair said, "They called you, Zeke. Go ahead and show your hand."

Zeke flipped his cards over. "Three jacks."

Jack Townsend showed his hand even though he didn't have to. "Two pair. Aces and sixes."

It was a polite game. Rusty George showed his hand, too. "Three tens. You drew out to beat me, Zeke."

Zeke smiled as he raked in the little pile of chips. "Just lucky, I guess." Before sorting out his chips he took the deck from Pete Bonair, cracked it on the table, split it, and started shuffling. "We'll play seven-card stud, one-eyed cowboy wild."

CHAPTER 9

Happy did not ride often, but he was a competent horseman and rode often enough to stay in condition. It was unusual but not incredible, then, when on Sunday afternoon he asked Gene if he might ride along with him at least part of the way to Walter Rose's place.

Gene was encouraged by the gesture and glad for the company, so he saddled a gentle bay gelding named Pepper, which was Happy's usual saddle horse. Happy knew well enough how to take care of his own horse, but it was a long-standing unspoken agreement that when Gene was free to saddle or hitch up horses for Happy, he did so, just as he put them away later. Similarly, it was understood that Gene could enjoy favors from the kitchen, such as an apple pie, or, more commonly, a few extras in the grub supply when Gene was on long rides or camp-outs. Neither of them kept tally of the favors, of course, because they were friends, and their reciprocal favors made life a little less austere in the bachelor world of Redboot.

The sun was shining warm and broad as they left headquarters. When they were out of earshot of the buildings, Happy came at his subject from a wide-angle arc. "That youngster Tommy Tipton seems to be working out just fine."

"Sure seems like it."

"Good-natured kid. Does his job, doesn't complain, minds his own business."

"Uh-huh."

"He seemed pretty interested in the talk about Charlie."

"Did he? I didn't notice."

"He didn't say much because he didn't have much to say. But he was paying attention."

"I can imagine why he might be interested, steppin' into Charlie's place as he did."

"It was an interesting discussion."

"I guess so."

"What part did you find most interesting?"

"I suppose it was the part about the marks on the throat."

"Bruise, but no matter. Do you want to know what part I found most interesting?"

"Go ahead. Tell me."

"The part about the shirt and the ground being wet."

"Why was that so interesting?"

"I imagine it was because it told me something about the underside of the case."

Gene stopped his horse and looked at Happy, who had also stopped. "You mean to tell me you think I know something about how Charlie died."

Happy shrugged. "Or how he got there."

"Or both."

"Or both."

They moved the horses forward again.

"Was it as obvious to the other fellas around the table?"

"I don't think so. And by that I don't mean that I'm so much the shrewder. It's just that nobody else knew about the shots that were fired at Zeke, or about Charlie's tendency not to be where he was supposed to be."

"That makes sense. Without those details, it would seem that Charlie had a general grudge against Zeke but wasn't doing much about it."

"My other clue, if you will, has been your own behavior. Since the day Charlie died, you've pulled a veil over you, Gene."

"Has it been that obvious?"

"Maybe not to people who don't know you as well, but I haven't missed it. So tell me, how did Zeke kill Charlie?"

"That's a pretty damn straight question." Gene licked his lips.

"Did he?"

"Yes, he did." Gene paused, choosing his words, and then he continued. "It was a terrible thing to see, Happy. There was an unbelievable . . . power, I guess. You could tell that somebody was likely to get killed. Charlie was fighting . . . savagely, that's all I can call it. At one point he tried gouging Zeke's eye out, and Zeke went wild, and he didn't stop until Charlie was finished. I tell you, it could've gone either way, but Zeke ended up on top."

"Just lucky, I guess."

Gene let out a short, nervous laugh. "Yeah, just lucky."

"Where did this gruesome event take place?" Happy asked, maintaining his ironic tone.

"Right there on Feather Creek, where we made such a mess of things with Bad Oscar. Same place, right afterwards."

"Charlie followed you there?"

"Yeah, he showed up there."

"And then you packed him down south here — I presume the two of you did — and then skeedaddled back?"

"I really wish we hadn't done it that way, Happy. But everything was out of kilter. We had just had the disaster with the bull, and then the fight, and it was startin' to rain. We were both washed out by it all, and it seemed like the easiest way at the time."

"I bet it was Zeke's idea."

"Well, yeah."

"And now you're an accomplice. The other way, you would have merely been a witness."

"That's about it."

"I'm sorry that it happened like that, Gene. It looks like your brother has gotten you into a bad spot."

"It kinda looks that way."

They rode on for a little while in silence, the horse hooves clopping and the saddles creaking. Then Happy spoke again. "There's a good chance that more will come of this."

"That's what I'm afraid of."

105

"But there might be one good effect. Of the secrecy."

"What would that be?"

"It will give brother Chet less grounds for starting trouble with Zeke."

"That's a good way to look at it."

"We take what we can get."

They rode on yet a while longer without talking. Then Gene spoke. "Well, Happy, I appreciate being able to clear this with you."

"Glad we did."

"Did you want to ride much further? I don't want to take you too far out of your way."

"Don't be foolish. I've come this far. I want to go the rest of the way with you, so I can meet your princess of the prairie." Happy smiled broadly at Gene. "How long did you think you could keep her to yourself, anyway?"

"I guess I just wasn't thinkin'," Gene bantered back.

"You're forgiven."

Gene chuckled and shook his head. Happy was in good humor, despite the somberness of their earlier conversation. Gene felt as if part of his burden was lifted now that he had shared it with someone he could trust. In addition, it helped to have another perspective on the situation, a viewpoint less full of dread than his own.

He looked at Happy, rocking slowly in the saddle as Pepper stepped along. The ranch cook did not cut much of a cowboy figure, with the corn-silk hair protruding beneath the broad-brimmed hat, and the firm paunch not quite bulging over the belt. He was his own man, that was for sure. One of a kind, thought Gene, and he was confident that Katharine and Happy would hit it off well.

As they approached, Katharine was watering cedar trees, little ones she had planted as a windbreak on the northwest side of the ranch house. She saw the riders a half mile away and waved. Even at that distance, Gene's heart was stirred, and a butterfly flapped in his stomach.

As they rode up and dismounted, she greeted them. "Good afternoon."

They both returned the greeting. Then Gene said, "Katharine, this is Owen Pollard, also known as Happy, master chef and bunkhouse bully of the Redboot."

Katharine laughed and her eyes sparkled.

"And Happy," Gene went on, "this is Katharine Rose." He wanted to add, "princess of the prairie," but the poetic spirit was not as strong in him as in Happy.

Katharine extended her hand. "I'm pleased to meet you, Happy."

The cook had removed his hat and now took her hand. "Pleased to meet you, Miss Rose."

From the way that neither seemed urgent to withdraw a hand, and from the feeling in the air, Gene sensed a friendship in the making.

"Just Katharine, please."

"Katharine with a *K?*" A release of the hands.

"Yes, with a *K*."

"Comes from the Greek word meaning 'pure.' *Katharos*."

Katharine blushed beneath her tan. "Do you know Greek, Happy?"

"No, I don't. I picked that up from reading a poet named John Milton. He knew Greek."

"Gene has said some nice things about his friend Happy, the bunkhouse bully," she said, winking at Gene.

"And he has said some delightful things about you. So I decided that today I would ride over with him and meet you for myself."

"I'm glad you did."

"So am I. And now, I think, it's time for me to be heading back."

Katharine smiled at him. "Are you sure you wouldn't like to stay for a while?"

"Another time. I need to get back and put some bread in the oven."

"Well, I'll let you go then. It's been nice meeting you."

"And nice meeting you." He tipped his hat, pulled himself into the saddle, and rode away.

Katharine held out her hands and Gene took them. He glanced toward the house and kissed her quickly.

She turned to look at the retreating figure of Happy on horseback, and then she turned back to Gene, smiling, and said, "I like him."

"Yes, he's a fine fellow. And a good friend." Then he looked at the empty buckets where she had set them when her visitors rode up. "Looks like we caught you in the middle of a job."

"I've got a few more left to water. You can help me if you'd like."

"Only if I get to carry the buckets."

"I'll tell you what, Gene. You carry them full, and I'll carry them empty."

"That sounds fair."

She picked up the two bucket handles with her left hand. Gene, leading Dodger with his right hand, felt his free hand meeting hers. Holding hands lightly, they walked back to the yard, with the light prairie breeze in their faces.

When they had finished watering the trees, they sat again in the shade of the cottonwood, his right knee almost touching her left. Occasionally their hands met as they talked about this small thing and that.

At one point she asked an unexpected question. "Do you like your work, Gene?"

He realized he had never thought of it that directly. "Well, yes, I suppose I do, now that I think about it. Why?"

"Not everybody does."

"Does your father?"

"Most of the time, I think."

"Do you?"

"Oh, yes. But then again, I'm not as driven to it as he is."

"Meanin' you have more choice. There are things you don't have to do if you don't want to."

She nodded. "Something like that. So it's easy for me to like what I do."

"I suppose I'm like your dad, then. I like what I do, most of the time." Then he had a glimmering of what might be the real question. "I don't think I'll go on workin' for wages forever, though."

"No?" Her earnest face showed her interest.

"No, I think eventually I'll want to file on my own place, get a few head of my own, and start a herd." He looked at her and smiled. "Register my own brand, too, y'know."

She pressed her hand into his. "That sounds exciting. It sounds just right for you, Gene. Tell me," she said, as her words quickened, "what's your idea of the best kind of place? Down on the plains, or up in the mountains?"

"Well, I like 'em both. I've seen some real fine layouts up there — ranch house and buildings in a nice mountain valley, trees and runnin' water and all." His glance traveled toward the mountains and then back. "But take it all around, day in and day out, year in and year out, I think I'd be more at home down here. There's trees and water here too, just farther apart."

"I hope you didn't say that just for me." Her head was lowered and she looked up at him. "That you like it better here."

He leaned over, pressed his left hand on her cheek, and kissed her. Then he settled back and said, "No, that's the way I feel. But maybe you're one of the reasons I feel that way."

"Well," she said, smiling and taking on her teasing air, "who am I to try to talk you out of that?"

"You know who you are. You're that pretty girl

110

down south that Gene Hill is crazy about."

"And all I have to do is crook my little finger," she said, doing just that as she wrinkled her nose.

They both laughed and joined hands again. Her hand felt warm and assuring.

Gene picked at the grass with his free left hand. "That's the picture," he said. "A little ranch, and a snug little cabin — or a bigger one, if need be," he corrected. He took on a mock-serious tone. "Man wouldn't want to live by himself forever."

She smiled faintly, matching his tone. "Man shouldn't."

Then he took a deep breath, and he could tell she could tell he was serious again. "Doesn't it seem sometimes like we each have our own destiny, and all we have to do is find it out? And then go after it?"

She nodded lightly. "Sometimes it seems that way."

He shrugged. "And mine seems to be the little ranch and ranch house down the trail." He looked at her. "And what do you think yours seems to be?"

"Well, I do have my own picture, but it's not quite as detailed as yours." She paused.

"Uh-huh . . ." Gene wondered, for the first time, if she would want to go on living where she was. He winced inwardly at the thought of trying to make even as good a living as Walter Rose did from this rough land. "Do you see yourself stayin' on here?"

"No," she said slowly. "This has been a good

place for Daddy, but he'll be the first to tell you he wouldn't have been able to make it off the land itself. He's had his horses, and that's what has helped carry him — us — through."

Gene nodded. "Seems that way from the outside, too."

"When Daddy's through with the place," she said, picking her words carefully, "it will probably get sold to Redboot."

"Where's that leave you?"

"Well, it's not going to happen tomorrow."

"No, but you said you had a picture."

"Well, yes. You have a clear picture of your place in the world. My picture of that is a little hazier." She paused as she bit her lip, and then she smiled and went on, "But I see myself at peace with the world."

"You mean not having any turmoil, not bein' hounded by other people, and such." Then Gene reflected that this was what he meant by peace.

"Well, that, of course. I couldn't go near a city for very long."

You can find turmoil at home, Gene thought. But he said, "Neither could I."

She picked up where she had left off. "But I also mean the kind of peace you find when you know you're in touch with — well, everything, I suppose. The animals, the trees, the flowers, the grass, the land, even the wind when it blows so long and hard. That's the kind of peace I mean, and I think I could find it in just about any place. Here, or over there" — she pointed toward

112

Redboot — "or up there." She pointed toward the mountains. Then she fell silent, as if she felt she had said too much.

"To have a place and be at peace," Gene said softly after a short while. "Those two go together nicely."

"They're not all that separate, are they?" she responded.

"No, they mean each other, sort of. Once you think of them together, it's hard to think of them separately."

"Like a boy and a girl," she said, tapping her finger on his nose.

"Like a boy and a girl," he repeated, as they drew close for another kiss.

"Or a man and a woman," she said, drawing her breath.

"Or a man and a woman."

CHAPTER 10

On the way home, Gene felt better than he had felt in a couple of weeks. He was relieved to have brought things out in the open to the extent that he had done so with Happy, and he felt he was on the right trail with Katharine. Conversation with her was always comfortable. As he was riding home, however, Gene did not feel right about still hiding his crime from her. And crime was what he had to call it, if he was going to be honest with himself.

Sharing his knowledge with Happy did not implicate him. It was no burden to Happy; it was essential information for him to act as detached observer and Gene's friend. That was clear from the way Happy had solicited and received the information.

But at this point, it seemed to Gene, that same knowledge would be a burden to Katharine. Eventually, if their lives came together as he hoped they would, he would come clean about it all. But for the time being, that gate remained closed. Neither of them had said anything about it during the visit, and from this distance he admired her for her well-mannered restraint. She had respected his need for privacy, while he, in feeling that need, also knew it was not right.

So he rode home across the warm and spreading plains, mostly happy in his heart from the day's events, but not without a tinge of sadness.

Zeke came riding in as Gene was putting away Dodger and checking on Pepper and the tack. Satisfied that everything was in order, Gene found a stem of hay to chew on and then lounged against a center post in the barn as Zeke took care of Bucky.

"How did things go on the Rose Ranch?"

"Rosy."

Zeke made a series of kissing sounds. "Must be wonderful to be in love. Young love."

"Oh, it is. You should try it."

"Saw Happy ride out with you."

"He just rode there and turned around and came back. I introduced him to my lady friend."

"Prob'ly diggin' for information."

"He was." Gene drew the sweet green taste out of the chewed hay stem.

For all his recklessness, Zeke had one careful habit that amused Gene. He always walked around to the off side of the horse, picked up the loose cinches, and laid them across the saddle. Zeke didn't like flopping cinches. Once, picking up a saddle he had dumped on the ground, he had jerked the saddle to fling the cinches, hoping they would drape just so over his arm. But he had fooled himself, and the buckle of the rear cinch came whipping around his thigh before he straightened up, and the buckle slapped him in the back of the testicles. "Sharper than the toe of a boot," he had told Gene at the time. Ever since then, he had been careful with his saddle.

Zeke pulled the saddle and double blanket from the horse. Over his shoulder he asked, "Did he get any?"

"I provided some."

Zeke came back from putting the saddle on its rack. "That's up to you, I guess. I'm not sure I would've said anything."

"He's been following it pretty closely from the start."

"I knew that."

"He had a good idea of what happened anyway." Gene glanced at the open barn door, which looked out on the afternoon shadow of the barn. Then, lowering his voice, he said, "He also explained that the way things worked out, we might be less likely to have trouble with Chet."

"Uh-huh. That makes sense." Zeke was brushing the horse now.

Gene attempted to brighten the conversation. "And how did things go in town?"

"Oh, all right."

Gene imitated the kissing sounds Zeke had made earlier.

"Not quite," Zeke said.

"She was home, wasn't she?"

"Oh, yeah. Just not alone."

"Someone else there?"

"Yeah. Henry Bransford. I couldn't get him out

of there with a crowbar."

"There's worse company."

"Oh, yeah. And I did pick up one interesting tidbit from him."

"What's that?"

"Chet Bickford is in town."

Gene felt a lurch in the pit of his stomach. "We knew he'd be here sooner or later," he said.

The other hands were sitting down at the table when Gene and Zeke came in. The brothers hung their hats, rinsed and dried their hands, and walked through the open doorway that led to the eating area. Usually the men ate an early supper on Sunday, so the lamps were not lit yet and the late afternoon sun streamed in through the west windows.

"We've got an extra guest this evening," Happy announced.

Gene chilled. "Oh, really? Who would that be?"

"Heel flies," said Jack Townsend.

"What's that?" Tommy Tipton asked.

"Another word for lawmen," Jack said.

"Sheriff Rolfe will be back any time," Happy clarified.

"Oh," Gene said blankly as he pulled out a chair. He kept from looking at Zeke.

"He visited with the boys a little while this afternoon," Happy went on. "Then he went out to look at the range, and he promised to be back for supper. I'm sure he'll keep his word."

"I'm sure he will," Jack said. "Two things them heel flies like — free food and free coffee."

"Clean it up, now," Happy said. "He could walk in any minute."

It wasn't many minutes before the sheriff did walk in. Gene knew Wilbur Rolfe, but he took the opportunity now to take a closer look. Rolfe was in his middle fifties, a man of average height and average build, not yet gone to seed and probably not likely to. He had a reputation for being in good condition, always ready for demanding hikes in rough country when his work took him there. He wasn't known for being quick with his fists or with a gun, but everybody knew he was firm and thorough. If he said something, he meant business. He didn't look tough, but his easy looks probably helped him get things done. With a full head of hair usually trimmed neatly above the ears and collar, a full bushy mustache, and friendly, smiling brown eyes, he had an easy manner that would do honor to a saloon-keeper or tobacconist. The latter would seem to fit him well, as he was very fond of his pipe. Gene imagined the sheriff having cultivated that aspect of his leisurely manner to better approach his fellow man in conversation. And it was known that Sheriff Rolfe chatted with everybody, heard much, and forgot nothing.

The sheriff sat down. He stuffed his pipe in the left pocket of his leather vest and looked at his pocket watch. "Just in time, I see," he said in an obvious bit of humor directed at himself. Then he looked around the table, smiling, and greeted the men he hadn't talked to that afternoon. "Hello,

Gene. Hello, Zeke. I see you're back in the country."

"Been back for a while."

"I think I might have heard that. And how are you likin' this country?" he asked of Tommy Tipton.

"I like it just fine."

"Your cook takin' good care of you?"

"Just fine. No complaints," the lad answered.

"Been killin' many snakes out the way you ride?"

"Some."

"I saw half a dozen of 'em on my little ride out there this afternoon."

"Did you kill any?" asked Jack Townsend.

The sheriff smiled. "Naw. I just go around 'em."

"I kill every one I see," Zeke said. "I don't like snakes, not one bit."

My God, Zeke, Gene thought. Can't you ever keep quiet?

"Me neither," said Pete Bonair. "You see these fellas with snakeskin hatbands and belts and such, but I'd just as soon have nothin' to do with 'em."

"Snakes, or men that fool around with 'em?" the sheriff asked.

"Both."

"They don't bother me that much," Zeke said, "but I don't like 'em."

The talk died down as Happy set platters of fried steaks and potatoes on the table. Then he came back with two tin plates of biscuits.

Gene looked at the biscuits. "I thought you were making bread."

Happy looked at him blankly. "No."

"You said you were making bread."

"When?"

"When you were out at the Roses' with me."

"Oh, that." Happy smiled. "I just wanted to leave you lovebirds alone."

"That tells you something about Happy," said the sheriff.

"What's that?" asked Zeke.

The sheriff raised his eyebrows as he speared a steak. "He wouldn't make a good liar."

"Why not?" asked Happy, as if defending his honor.

"A good liar remembers which lies he told, when, and who to." The sheriff looked around, as if he expected at least a ripple of laughter. Then he went on. "But I'll tell you one thing Happy can't lie to us about."

"What's that?" asked Zeke.

"I sat here drinkin' coffee this afternoon and watched him roll out the dough for two pies. And you can bet I'm not goin' back to town without passin' judgment on at least one of them. No-sir."

"I believe you," said Jack.

The sheriff smiled and salted down his steak. Then there was no talk at all, just the clack of silverware on plates, the shifting of a body in a chair, the soft clunk of a coffee mug being set on the table.

After supper had been done justice and the dirty

plates and utensils were stacked in the wreck pan, Happy sat back down at the table.

"I think I'll save the dishes till later," he said. "I'll join the sheriff in a pipe."

"Have you got enough plates and forks for the pie later on?" asked Rolfe, pausing as he drew out his pipe.

"Of course," said Happy. "I've got enough for a whole roundup crew and then some."

"Then I won't worry."

Everyone else kept to their chairs as well, pushing away from the table to hike one leg on another or to sprawl. Zeke rolled and lit a cigarette, as did Pete Bonair, who also smoked. Tommy Tipton seemed fascinated by a steel-handled penknife of the sheriff's, which had a short blade and not much of a point. It looked well suited to the sheriff's purpose of carefully scraping out the bowl of his pipe.

Sheriff Rolfe, apparently noting Tommy's interest, held up the knife between thumb and forefinger and said, "I bought this in a shop in Denver that sells nothing but knives."

Tommy raised his eyebrows and nodded.

"Well, Sheriff," said Zeke, "we're all just dyin' to hear about your errand out this way."

"I'm sure you are." The sheriff stuffed a large pinch of dark, stringy tobacco into his pipe. "And I'm not much of a mystery man. Chet Bickford is in town."

"I think I might have heard that," Zeke said, deadpan.

The sheriff's eyebrows flicked as if in recognition of the mimicry, but he didn't acknowledge it. "And, as you might imagine, he's concerned about what happened to his brother."

A general nod of assent went around the table.

"Naturally, he's tried to lean on me," the sheriff continued, striking a match.

"What about?" demanded Jack Townsend — somewhat curtly, it seemed to Gene, until he recalled that Jack had not shown much fondness for heel flies or for Charlie.

"Well, the details themselves" — the sheriff puffed — "the details" — he struck another match — "of Charlie's death are well known and have been thoroughly discussed in the saloons around town."

Gene felt an inward spread of dismay.

"So Chet is curious. He's heard that his brother was apparently thrown from his horse in a gentle rainstorm and was not wearing a jacket. His shirt was wet before he fell, and somewhere along the way he acquired a bruise on his throat."

"So Chet sent you out here to investigate?" asked Jack.

Apparently the sheriff hadn't talked about Chet, just Charlie, during his afternoon visit.

"I wouldn't put it that way," said the sheriff, as he admired the thick, rich cloud of smoke he had just blown out. "I came out here to look things over and gain a few impressions for myself, not that there's anything new to see. I verified a few details with you boys, and my thanks again for that."

"You should've rode over to Roses' and asked how bad it was stormin' that day," said Rusty George, who still seemed to consider himself an authority on the case.

"I found time for that," said the sheriff. "Apparently I just missed you, Gene," he said, nodding in his direction. "I got to talk to his pretty daughter. It was a calm rain there, too."

At the mention of Katharine, Gene felt himself go weak.

"At any rate," said the sheriff, returning his gaze to Jack Townsend, "I thought I would come out here on my own and try to discourage Chet from takin' things upon himself unnecessarily."

"He'll be out here anyway," said Jack. "He has to pick up Charlie's gear and horse."

"Yes, he'll be here," answered the sheriff, "but now he'll understand he doesn't have a free hand in the case."

"I know him," said Zeke. "He's just as much trouble as his brother."

Rolfe took the pipe from his mouth and looked at Zeke. "His brother was killed. He doesn't know how. He has a right to satisfy himself on that, just as you would — beg your pardon, Gene."

"Quite all right."

The sheriff looked around the table. "That more or less sums it up." His gaze settled on the cook. "And now, Happy, if it's not too early, how about some of that apple pie you tried to hide from us, while we're still all gathered here?"

"Coming right up," Happy said readily. "Clean plates and all."

Good, thought Gene. He wants to get back to town.

The sheriff ate his slab of pie without comment until he was finished. Then, laying his fork on his plate but not pushing his plate away, he blew the steam off his freshly filled coffee mug, took a sip, and said, "That was first-rate, Happy."

"Glad you liked it."

"Glad you had enough for me."

"With six hands in the bunkhouse, I have to make two pies or go without myself." He looked at the sheriff with a pained expression. "I hate the idea of cutting a pie into more than six pieces."

"Terrible thing to do to a pie," said the sheriff, glancing at the remaining half-pie in what seemed to Gene to be a moment of relaxed self-control.

"Would you like a second piece?" offered the cook.

"Not right now, thank you. Maybe later." The sheriff settled into his chair and took another drink of coffee, then took up his pipe again and relit it.

"Leave your plates there, boys," Happy said to the others, who had all finished. "We'll have seconds in a little while and clean it up."

Gene grasped what Happy had apparently already sensed, that the sheriff might have more to say.

But he didn't seem to. Instead, he listened pleasantly to an idle round of talk about Henry

Bransford and his plan to have a telephone system.

"That's what you need, sheriff," declared Rusty George. "A telephone."

"Oh, I'd be tickled to death to have one," he said, and then he lapsed into silence.

Presently the talk came around to summer range and who might be sent to the mountain, and on to the inevitable talk of cabin fever and sheepherders who went loco.

"Reminds me of a story they tell about a couple of boys in Idaho," the sheriff said. Then, seeing that he had their attention, he went on. "Miners, these two fellas. Seems they had some trouble with another man jumpin' their claim, and they felt obligated to kill him at some point. Well, as the story goes, they took him down to a wide spot in the river. They built a dam out of rocks, diverted the stream, dug a hole in the river bottom, tossed the man in there and covered him with rocks, and then turned the river back over him."

"Lotta work," said Rusty George.

"Yes, and all for nothing," continued the sheriff. "The next spring, the river changed course in that wide spot, and when the dead man's friends went lookin' for him, there they found him with his hand stickin' up between the rocks, as if he was tryin' to climb out. I guess the rocks had shifted with the motion of the water, and the body had shifted some, too."

Gene thought to say it was too bad the miners didn't get a chance to come back first and rebury the body, but he was haunted with the feeling that

125

the sheriff was telling the story partly for his benefit. So he didn't oblige Rolfe with a response.

No one else seemed to have a ready comment either. As if to close out the story with a "So what?" the sheriff said, "Yes-sir, strange doin's in the mountains."

The talk trailed away after that. Then everybody had another half piece of pie, and the sheriff was gone.

As the hoofbeats faded away, Jack Townsend sniffed and said, "Heel flies."

"Yeah, but I like him," Zeke said, rolling a cigarette one-handed and studying his work.

CHAPTER 11

As everybody expected, Chet Bickford did show up to collect his brother's belongings and to learn what he might. He rode in the very next day. Gene and Zeke, who had taken over the western range so that Pete Bonair and Rusty George could get things in order to go to the mountain, rode in at sundown to find Chet lounging in the bunkhouse.

When Gene saw him, he was struck by the resemblance to Charlie. Gene had met Chester Bickford in the past and had observed the similarity, but when he walked into the bunkhouse and saw him, it was as if he were seeing Charlie all over again. Chet was a little older, a little darker, and a little thicker in build than his late brother, and so he looked like a mature version of the sapling that had been cut down in green leaf.

Chet was red-haired and red-bearded, insofar as his stubble could be called a beard, but with the red shading more to brown than with Charlie. His hat was lying on the cold sheet-iron stove, so his balding spot, a chilling replica of his brother's, was visible as Gene walked in. Along his temples and thatching over his ears, below the hair that was flattened and slicked from the hat, Chet's wavy hair had a few strands of gray.

Never having been fast friends, the Hill brothers and Chet exchanged curt greetings. Zeke stretched out on his creaking bunk while Gene sat on the edge of his. Gene looked at Chet and remembered how the sheriff had admonished Zeke. "His brother was killed. He doesn't know how." Chet's face, like Charlie's, seemed to be a glowing opaque lens that held in, but allowed to shine through, a burning, full-fueled rage at the world. At the same time, Chet's flushed face seemed haggard and drawn, traced with the anguish and frustration of having lost a brother and not knowing why. Gene could feel the sadness that had to be blended with Chet's anger and bitterness. Gene could not bring himself to like Chet, but he found it in himself to say, "I'm sorry about Charlie."

"Everybody is," Chet snapped. He was chewing a toothpick, and he shifted it from the left side of his mouth to the right, mashing it with his teeth as he moved it across. The hinges of his jaw bulged just as they had in the younger Bickford.

Chet seemed to have, in addition to his imposing physical presence, the same arrogance that had been so evident in his brother. He seemed like a man who had come to settle a score and who expected to do it in his way, to his satisfaction. Then Gene noticed it, the one trait by which he could differentiate the two and not fall prey to the haunting sense that he was witnessing the return of a darker, uglier Charlie. The difference was that Chet's head stayed still; it did not sway or waggle like Charlie's. That was a good thing to notice, for it drove away some of the eeriness that had crept into the encounter.

The code of the cow country made Chet welcome as a supper guest and overnight lodger with no questions asked on either side. He seemed to be taking the code at full value, sprawled in comfort despite the tension that was so obvious and lay so near the surface. Even though he still wore his spurs, he had the aura of not being in a hurry to go anywhere until he felt like it. Gene saw the bedroll flung out on what had been Charlie's bunk (Tommy Tipton had avoided it, just as the others had) and he saw the war bag stuffed underneath. These details, coupled with Chet's proprietary air, told Gene that Chet assumed a right to stay on as he pleased. Gene hoped against fear that he would stay just the one night.

Conversation did not flow freely and lightly in the interval before supper. After Zeke had lain stretched out on his bunk for a while, he sat up on the edge of the bed and rolled himself a cigarette. Chet seemed to be moved by the power of suggestion and started to roll himself one also. He did not seem really to have noticed Zeke's action on a conscious level; he was too absorbed in his own project, though not doing nearly as slick a job of it as Zeke. He spilled tobacco on his shirt, and with no apparent thought he brushed it onto the floor. Gene heaved an inward sigh of relief, remembering how such a simple thing as a cigarette had sparked the first conflagration between Charlie and Zeke. Lighting his cigarette, Chet cracked the lid of the stove and tossed the match inside, first having shook it out. Then he pushed the lid open further with his toe, took a powerful drag on the cigarette, and flicked the end ash into the stove. None of his actions seemed to be performed for anyone's benefit, but for Gene, every gesture was full of menace.

Zeke, meanwhile, smoked his cigarette in oblivion, using a sardine can as an ashtray. Then he spoke. "They tell me you been workin' for a big outfit up Kaycee way, Chet."

"Whoever 'they' are, they told you the truth," Chet said, leaving the unmistakable impression that Zeke might not be used to the truth.

"Just tryin' to make small talk."

"You did."

"Nothin' like a little comedy to shorten the time before supper," said Jack Townsend, who had been lying on his bunk and saying nothing since Gene and Zeke had come in.

Chet grunted.

Zeke raised his eyebrows in a gesture of futility, snuffed out his cigarette, and lay back down on his squeaky bunk.

Pete Bonair and Rusty George came in from outside, and from the way they nodded at Chet, Gene surmised they had become reacquainted earlier in the day. They seemed to avoid looking directly at Gene, which told him further that they likely had been talking about him. And brother Zeke.

Happy sounded the call for supper, and there was an immediate clumping of boots, scraping of chairs, and clattering of plates.

"Beans and biscuits," declared Pete Bonair as he sat down.

"Yep, and tomorrow, for variety, it's biscuits and beans," said Jack Townsend.

"Trouble with beans," said Zeke, "is they tend to talk behind your back."

Tommy Tipton laughed. "That's a good one. I haven't heard that one before."

"It's an old joke," scowled Chet. "You must not 'a been in the country long."

Supper settled down to be as cheerful as the earlier conversation. Then Happy spoke up. "I almost forgot." He went to the kitchen and brought back a small dish of violent-looking green peppers, short and stubby like nubbin carrots but sleek and dark as nightshade. He set them in front of Zeke. They looked potent, reposed in the oily fluid they had been pickled in.

"What's the juice?" Gene asked.

"*Escabeche*," Happy said, enunciating it clearly as a four-syllable word. "Vinegar and oil. And some of the oil is from the peppers themselves. What do you think, Zeke? I got a tin of them just for you."

"Ah likes 'em," said Zeke, flicking into an imitation of an unidentified source. He picked up a pepper by the stem, put it into his mouth, and pulled the stem free. "Mighty fine." He pushed

131

the bowl toward Chet. "Help yourself. Put lead in your pencil."

"Puts fire in your ass is what you mean," said Chet. "If that's your idea of a good time."

"You don't like a damn thing, do you?" pushed Zeke.

"I don't like you."

"You don't have to."

Happy, who had returned to his chair nearest the kitchen, gave a look that said neither of them had to like anything.

Zeke looked at the cook. "Sorry, Happy. Thanks for the peppers, too. They're the gen-u-wine stuff." He pushed the dish toward Tommy Tipton, who smiled and shook his head.

Then he pushed them toward Gene, who did not share his brother's fondness for hot peppers but who felt the urge to eat one. As he picked up the nearest pepper he felt Chet's eyes on him, and he knew that his impulse could not be separated from his resentment of Chet Bickford.

His lips, his tongue, the whole interior of his mouth — it all inflamed at once, burning and piercing. Tears started in his eyes. Sweat beaded on his forehead as he felt his face flush.

"How do you like 'em?" Zeke asked.

He found his voice and rasped, "Just right."

Everyone at the table, including Chet, laughed. Gene smiled, and as Zeke smiled and plucked another pepper from its dish, Gene knew in that moment he would always stick by his brother.

The meal went on. Plates got refilled, biscuits

got sopped in bean juice.

Even Chet Bickford seemed to appreciate the meal. "Good grub, Happy," he said.

Gene watched him eat, the enemy absorbed in fueling his fury. Sometimes Chet shoveled the spoon straight into his mouth, with his hand wrapped around the handle and his elbow elevated. Sometimes he worked it with his elbow down, holding the spoon aloft with his thumb under the handle and his fingers wrapped over it. Either way, he made short work of his food. Then Gene remembered where else he had seen a person holding a spoon with his thumb pushing up under the shank of the handle. It was at this same table, not a month ago.

Chet finished eating and pushed his plate away. Drawing a toothpick from the cup in the center of the table, he lapsed into picking his teeth sullenly.

Gene looked at Zeke, who was absent-mindedly balancing a toothpick lengthwise in the groove of his tongue and flicking it up and down, backward and forward, through the gap in his front teeth. Gene wanted to laugh. He was sure Zeke knew as well as he did that Chet would like to kill Zeke, dead and forever, if he could work up enough good reason. Yet here Zeke was, filling up the mealtime with good humor and boyish antics, never doubting that the moment might come. Between Chet's anger and Zeke's insouciance, there was a deadly humor to the scene, as if Zeke might think it a pretty good joke to give Chet Bickford the surprise of his life.

Happy went into the kitchen with the dirty dishes while the rest of the men sat around the table. Pete and Zeke rolled cigarettes, as did Chet.

Jack Townsend finally spoke. "Well, Rusty, you and Pete be takin' off to the mountain in the mornin', huh?"

Rusty, who had been unusually quiet, said, "Yep. Be nice to get up there an' smell the fresh breeze an' the pine trees. Sky allus seems bluer there, too."

Jack, still making conversation, said to Gene, "That leaves you and Zeke over west here, then, huh?"

"Looks like it," said Gene. Then he thought, thanks for tellin' Chet where he can find us. Gene looked at Chet, whose face registered attention to the details just passed.

Chet took a drag on his cigarette and exhaled. The seam of the paper was buckling apart where he had not rolled the smoke smoothly, so he took another long drag to burn past the flaw before the cigarette could fall apart.

Gene watched him, a seemingly thick-headed brute intent on making the best of his own clumsy work. Once again like his brother, Chet had a hard face to read. It always expressed discontent, anger frozen in the features. With some men, every emotion or feeling showed clearly; if a troubling thought wandered through the mind it showed on the face, just as a flash of amusement would brighten the face. With other men, only the most extreme emotions showed. Neither the chameleon face nor the stone face characterized Chet. Even if he had a pleasant thought, it did not show, or at least not clearly through the constant sheen of unhappiness. It seemed, however, as if Chet were trying to work himself into something resembling fellowship, as if he were practicing amiability on his cigarette.

"Have we got a deck of cards?" he asked. "We could have a few hands of poker before we turned in."

No one seemed excited. Pete and Zeke studied their cigarettes. Jack Townsend looked at Rusty George, who shrugged, and then at Tommy Tipton, who duplicated the shrug.

"We just had a game night 'fore last," said Rusty.

"Ain't every day you get strange money in for a walk-around," Chet wheedled. "Y'ought to jump on it."

"It's certainly gen'rous of you," said Pete Bonair, giving him a sideways glance.

"I like to spread my good will around," Chet answered, in an evident attempt to be cheerful.

Jack Townsend looked at Zeke, who looked intently at his cigarette.

"Oh, hell with y'all, then," said Chet. "It's all the same to me."

"I guess we can break out the chips for a while, boys?" said Jack, looking around. There was a general murmur of assent, so Jack went for the box of chips.

Chet got up to go to his war bag, and to Gene's surprise he came back with a full bottle of whiskey. Gene winced. It was generally understood that the men didn't drink on the ranch. It wasn't a hard and fast rule, but it was something that just didn't get done, especially on a Monday night.

Jack Townsend, who did not have a heroic resistance to liquor, looked surprised as he came to the table with the chips.

As usual, Gene sat back and watched the rest of them get the game under way.

"What do we play, open on jacks or open on guts?" Chet asked.

"Don't have to be neither," said Rusty. "Don't even have to be five-card. We play dealer's choice. Me, I usually deal five draw, open on guts, and Pete does too, but you can deal whatever you want."

"House rules," said Chet, by way of agreement. "I'd ruther play five-draw guts myself, but we'll play however y'all are used to."

"Standard rules," Jack said. "Table stakes, no check and raise, protect your hand, no string bets — what else, Rusty?"

"No whorehouse cuts or trash games."

"Okay. That, too." Jack looked at Chet. "Just normal poker."

By now the other players were in place. As Jack counted out chips, Chet took a pull on the bottle and started it around to his left, in the direction of the deal. Tommy turned his nose down at it and handed it to Rusty, who passed it to Jack.

The banker paused in his counting to take a swig. Then he handed it to Zeke, who passed and offered it to Gene and then Pete Bonair. Pete handed it to Chet.

Jack continued to count out chips. He handed the deck to Rusty George at his right, and the game got under way. Pete Bonair won the first two hands, both small pots of five-draw. Then the deal went to Zeke.

"We'll play seven-card stud, one-eyed cowboy wild," he said.

Chet paused with his fist around the neck of the whiskey bottle. "That ain't poker. That's a half-assed kitchen game if I ever heard one." He drank.

"We play it here," Zeke said as he shuffled.

Chet retipped the bottle for another drink. "I say it's a jack-off kitchen game, but we can play it. Shit," he said, handing the bottle across the table to Jack, "we can play Old Maid if you girls want to."

Jack cut the deck and took a drink. "No harm," he said. "Everyone knows how to fold." Then, not having missed a trick, he tipped himself a second drink, too.

Gene watched the game, somewhat surprised at Zeke's playing. His brother frittered away half his stack betting on two pairs, queens and sixes, which Gene knew was a poor hand in seven-stud with a wild card. Then he realized Zeke was trying to go bust to get out of the game. It pleased him that Zeke was showing good judgment.

Tommy Tipton won the hand, raising on Chet with every card and building a fair-sized pot, including a generous contribution from Zeke. Chet cast a look of resentment as the chips were dragged under his nose and into Tommy's territory.

Happy came from the kitchen and stood filling his pipe. Seeing the bottle, he wrinkled his nose but said nothing. Gene motioned with his head to go into the next room, which they did, leaving the eating area to the cardplayers. A few hands later, Zeke joined them.

"Busted out already?" asked Gene.

"Couldn't hold cards and couldn't buy a hand," Zeke said, putting on an air of complaint. He stretched and yawned, then lay down on his bunk.

"Why don't you read to us, Happy?" Gene suggested.

"I guess I could," said the cook. "What do you have a fancy for? Macbeth's soliloquy upon hearing the news of his wife's death?" He puffed on his pipe and winked. "Or Marc Antony's oration at the funeral of Julius Caesar?"

"Any of that," Gene said. "You know how I like it all."

Zeke shifted in his bunk. "Let's go light on the death and funeral business. How about a nice story about pretty young women?"

"I think I might be able to compromise," said Happy. He went to the bookshelf and pulled out a dark green book, which he carried with him back to his chair. After setting his pipe on the cold stove and clearing his throat, Happy opened the book and began to read:

Evangeline
by Henry Wadsworth Longfellow
"This is the forest primeval. The murmuring
pines and the hemlocks,
Bearded with moss, and in garments green,
indistinct in the twilight,
Stand like Druids of eld, with voices sad and
prophetic."

Happy hit a stride with the cadence of the lines,
and he wound himself up into an energetic reading
that must have caught the attention of the poker
players, for the rattle of chips and the table talk
fell silent as Happy declaimed.

"Ye who believe in the beauty and strength
of woman's devotion,
List to the mournful tradition still sung by
the pines of the forest;"

Here he paused, and the shuffle of cards announced the resuming of the poker game. Then,
holding the open book in the palm of his hand
and looking Gene and then Zeke in the eyes, he
proceeded into the story of the separated lovers.
Within a few minutes he came to the passage introducing the father of the heroine and then the
heroine herself. Like Walter Rose, Gene thought,
as Happy described the father and then the girl.
Old man, young daughter. As Happy read on,

Gene smiled at the description of the lovely maiden with blackberry eyes and beautiful brown hair. He could almost see that pretty girl right there. Maybe Happy had a good story after all.

Gene only half-heard the next several lines, telling of her procession to and from Sunday worship. He was still fixed on the gleaming eyes, dark hair, and smiling face. Then he came out of his reverie as Happy read the line: "When she had passed, it seemed like the ceasing of exquisite music."

Happy read on, eventually introducing Basil, the blacksmith, and Basil's son Gabriel, in love with Evangeline. The poker game was rattling along famously now, and Gene could hear the frequent squeak of the cork being pulled from the bottle. Then the tale darkened with the news that the happy peasants would all be deported, and then came the heartbroken death of the heroine's father, as the village burned in the background. It all seemed mournful to Gene, but Happy showed no signs of tiring, although he had been reading vigorously for nearly an hour. Then he read the line: "Leaving behind them the dead on the shore, and the village in ruins."

He paused, inclined his head slightly, and looked up. "It goes on," he said. "Shall we resume with Part the Second, or save it for another time?"

Suddenly the tranquility of the evening was shattered. Chairs scraped, poker chips rattled, and boots scrambled. There was the sound of scuffling and the jingle of spurs.

Gene looked around in time to see Chet dragging

Jack Townsend across the poker table beneath the swinging overhead lamp. He slammed Jack against the wall, where Jack slumped, no doubt weakened by fear and whiskey. Chet slapped him once, twice, three times, four — he wasn't stopping. Gene could not see the other men through the open doorway, but evidently no one was interfering.

Zeke, who had gotten quite relaxed by Happy's intonations, was up and awake. Without a word between them, Zeke and Gene bolted to the fight and pulled Chet away. Chet tore loose from them and turned, punching Gene square on the cheekbone. Gene stopped short, half-dazed and seeing spots. Zeke stood off wary, with his fists ready.

"I knew it, you sonsabitches," Chet said. "I knew you'd both jump me, just like you did Charlie."

Gene spoke without thinking. "Zeke fought him fair, one on one." Then fear crept through him as he realized what he had almost said.

Chet's face flamed in rage as the lamplight waved on his face. "You're a coward and a liar both. Don't deny it. Everyone knows. The two of you ganged up on Charlie, and then your chickenshit brother here kicked him in the face." Chet was quivering. "Don't try it with me." He waved a shaky hand. "Don't even come near me. I'll kill you. I'll kill you both."

"You're not goin' to kill anybody," Zeke said.

CHAPTER 12

All the men went to their bunks shortly after the ruckus, but not before Gene had gotten a whispered explanation from Pete Bonair. Jack had passed a remark about Chet's ill humor, and he had made the blunder of saying something to the effect that Chet was as much of a sourpuss as his brother had been. Then Chet exploded, the fight followed, and an uneasy truce arrived.

In the morning, Monte came to the bunkhouse. Usually he kept to his own quarters, especially in the evening. If he came at all it was in the morning, usually a winter morning. This morning's visit was out of the ordinary.

He came in while the men were turning out of bed. It was still dark outside. "You, Chet," he said. "You roll your blankets, and you get what you came for, and you rowel out of here. Don't come back, and don't let me hear of you bein' anywhere on the Redboot range. And I mean it." Monte was a short, hatchet-faced man who seldom said much of anything. He kept to himself, gave terse orders, and didn't have much to say about how a job got done. He might ride two hours or two days to take a look at how the work was faring, and he was likely as not to turn around and ride back to the ranch without so much as a word. But this morning he had some to say. "Your brother was a good hand, but he got in trouble. He didn't always do what he was told, but when he did, he did good. You've never worked for me, and you won't. So you just have one chance to do what you're told. Get off and don't come back." Monte turned to leave and then he paused at the doorway. "Pete and Rusty, you stay down here on the range. Gene and Zeke, you two go to the mountain. You stay there till I say so." Then Monte left the bunkhouse.

Gene went into the kitchen and poured himself a cup of coffee. Happy, who was always up well ahead of the hands, looked at Gene and gave a shrug.

Gene, realizing that Happy had gone to tell Monte about the flare-up, said, "I don't blame you. You can't have that goin' on in your bunkhouse. I say good riddance."

Happy nodded. "I hope so."

Gene took the coffeepot with him to the table, where he sat down in the lamplight. Chet already had his bedroll and war bag ready, and he was paused to put his hat on before going outside. "You'd just as well stay for breakfast, Chet," Gene said.

"I wouldn't have it in my ass if I had room for a sawmill," he answered.

Happy spoke from behind Gene. "You might as well have breakfast, Chet. We just had a bad incident, that's all. There's no need for hard feelings."

"I've got no hard feelin's against you, Happy, but I can't say the same for some of your friends. So it's best I rowel out, as your boss said. I done wore out my welcome here."

"Well enough, Chet. Good luck."

"Thanks, Happy." And Chet Bickford walked out.

"How about Charlie's gear?" Gene asked.

"He sorted it out yesterday afternoon," Happy said. "It's in the barn with his saddle, all ready to go, I imagine."

By the time all the punchers got sat down to the table and the platter of hotcakes went around, good nature was on the rise again. Then they heard the clip-clop of two horses leaving the yard.

"There goes one unhappy man," said Pete Bonair.

Nobody else said anything, but Gene was sure there were others thinking as he did, that they hadn't seen the last of Chet.

It took some rearranging and repacking to get Gene and Zeke sent off in place of Pete and Rusty. The four of them were to drive the herd from the northwest part of the ranch to the lower ranges on the mountain. From then on, Gene and Zeke would push the cattle from one part of the mountain to another, grazing the prime meadows and open hillsides. It was a full day's drive this first day, starting at daybreak, and by the time they got their changes made, the sun was climbing in the sky and the morning was wasting.

To go see Katharine was out of the question. The best he could do was scrawl a quick note and explain the unexpected change in plans. He also included in his note the suggestion that she could get in touch with him through Happy. Then, as a gesture of confidence to Tommy Tipton, he asked the lad to deliver the letter for him.

All the way to the mountain, Gene felt disappointed in the course of events, and he also regretted not being in the frame of mind to enjoy what he was doing. There was a time when he would have rejoiced at being able to go to the mountain, but today he was going because he had caused trouble and needed to be sent out of the way. It was also a punishment unintended on Monte's part, for it would keep Gene separated from Katharine just at a time when they were growing closer together.

In addition to his dismay over the circumstances, he was chagrined that some of the zest of life had been knocked out. He was in love with a woman with whom he could be absolutely open, and yet he had to hide some of the truth from her. Also, he was anxious to know about her conversation with Sheriff Rolfe. He doubted that Rolfe had ferreted out the knowledge of the sniping in the broken country, and yet he could not be sure. He would just have to live with that anxiety until he got a chance to clear it up.

Over all of these drab misgivings hung the cloud of Chet Bickford. Monte had told him well enough to stay clear, yet he knew where he could find Gene and Zeke, which he would have known either way. Chet was primed for retaliation, and his visit to the bunkhouse had only served to put more powder in the pan.

Going to the mountain was no vacation, but generally it was looked upon as an opportunity for freedom and relaxation — what Katharine would call peace with the world, Gene thought. On the mountain, a man was at large with the surroundings, detached and out of touch from the network of daily doings. It was as if the mountain and Henry Bransford's telephone were not even in the same life. The mountain was a world unto itself, and now it too was spoiled by the worries Gene brought with him as surely as the packs on the packhorses. Not least among those worries was the realization that the mountain held an infinite number of hidey-holes and sniper nests.

Gene wished he could have life the way it was meant to be — just he and his brother, their remuda of work horses, and a herd of cows and calves, all going to the mountain. He thought of what a fine life it would be if just he and Katharine were going to the mountain, with or without cattle to tend. Even if he were by himself, or even riding herd with Jack Townsend, in another time he would have been able to expand his spirit among the rocks and the eagles, go out of himself if only for a few moments. But all of that was spoiled on this trip, made bitter by the realization that he had spoiled it for himself.

Cow camp on the mountain started out at the base camp, which consisted of a rough cabin, a lean-to for horses in bad weather, and a casual corral. From there, as the herd moved back and forth and higher up the mountain, the boys lodged in a canvas wall tent, much like those used in military campaigns. Life was free-flowing, as they stayed sometimes in the tent and sometimes in the cabin.

They got to the cabin late that first night. Pete and Rusty stayed over, and the next morning after breakfast they saddled their horses in the crisp morning air and rode away.

"See you when the snow flies," Pete joshed.

"Don't let the sound of the choo-choo trains get to you," Rusty George said.

It was a standing joke. Some years back, a wool grower had brought an army of his grass maggots to this country, and he had pastured a sizable herd of them up here on the mountain, in the care of a sheepherder. After a couple of months the boss came up to fetch supplies and to see how loony his sheepherder had gotten. In conversation the herder made it known that he didn't mind the solitude, even when it stormed terrible, but he was bothered some by the frequent noise of choo-choo trains. There was not a railroad within a two-day ride.

"Know what I herd, Rusty?" Zeke asked.

"What's that?" Rusty asked, always on the look-out for a stray scrap of gossip.

"Cattle, not sheep." Zeke laughed.

Gene laughed. That must have been the tenth time Rusty fell for that joke.

"So long, fellas," Zeke said to Pete and Rusty. "Don't forget to kiss the cook."

Life did settle down and smooth out on the summer range, even if it was not as perfect and free as a fellow might want it to be. The daily routine was simple — make meals, tend to camp chores, herd cattle, and sleep. There was very little in the way of equipment, so all tasks were simple and primitive. Except for the base camp, there was no human structure or pattern imposed on the landscape — no fences, no geometry of roads, no buildings, no groups of buildings. Life was not entirely random, but it followed the more natural patterns of watercourses, ridges and valleys, cow trails and game trails, and the daily movement of the sun. The men followed the cattle, and the cattle followed the contours of the land, the availability of water, and the warmth and shade given by the sun.

When the pasturing was far enough from base camp they pitched the tent. Then when they struck camp, preparatory to moving back to base camp or to another spike camp, it gave Gene a good feeling to see the bare campsite, having cast off its human trappings and gone back to itself. It was reassuring to know that something as useful as a camp could be rolled up and packed in the panniers of a packhorse, meanwhile not having done any harm or left any dents in the landscape.

There was always the fire pit, of course — the

one small blemish. Usually they camped in a place where a camp had been pitched before, and so they used the pit that was already there. Over several years' time, if it was not used again, it would blow over with dust and grow over with grass, but in the meanwhile it did show the mark of man, the only fire-building animal.

It would be nice to live completely primitive, without even a tent, but that would be folly in this country. A rainstorm was likely to build up on any day, more often in the afternoon than in the morning, but possible at any time. If a man was ever to have dry flour, bedding, or extra socks, a shelter of some kind was imperative.

Through the rest of the year, especially when the winter wind howled and drove snowdrifts on the plains, this life came to memory as an unbroken series of sunny afternoons in broad meadows and dappled timber. But in reality, the weather could change a half dozen times in a day, vacillating from fragile warmth to creeping chill as the clouds built and then hung or moved out. Sometimes the sunny warmth would persist for days in a row, but it was also characteristic for this place to be shrouded in mists for a day or more. Most of the cattle they had brought to the mountain were cows with calves, but there were a few bulls in the herd. On misty days the bulls seemed to bellow the most, maybe because of their clouded sense of direction. Then again, Gene thought, maybe it just seemed that way because the bellowing carried strangely in the moist air and reverberated against the wet canyon walls. More than once he thought of Bad Oscar.

On some evenings the brothers could sit outside by the campfire, gazing at the open sky and listening to the yelp and howl of coyotes. On other nights they were kept inside the tent for close fellowship amid the smell of burning candle wax, wet wool socks, muddy trousers, and damp wood-smoky jackets. It was good fellowship, though, working and joking through life with the person whose life came from the same place. And the sun always broke out, sooner or later, to air out and dry out all the things that got close inside a tent.

Gene and Zeke talked about their boyhood and growing up on the Platte, about women, about cattle and horses, about the men they knew and worked with, sometimes about Chet Bickford and even less about Charlie. Gene occasionally wondered how Zeke, with more at stake in the business, could manage to seem so unconcerned. He had killed a man and lied about it, and he might well have to answer to the man's deadly brother, and yet he did not seem to be immensely bothered. It was as if he followed the chain of problems link by link, back to the place at which he was most justified in what he did. That could be Zeke's good fortune, if he lived to leave this country — his ability to slough off guilt.

It was not all cloud and gloom. On sunny days, especially when Gene was off by himself, away from camp and without any cows in sight, he could let himself go. He would sit with his back against a tree or a rock, with the reins trailing slack through an open hand, and let the small sounds of the natural world fill in around him. Then he went out of himself — not entirely as if he had eaten forest mushrooms, but just enough to feel like part of the immediate world around him. He did not succeed in becoming the rock or the tree, as Indians were said to do in certain states of mind, but he did succeed in becoming more than Gene Hill, a cowhand encased in stinking flannels, denim, and leather. He flowed through his garments like heat through a blanket or light through a tent wall, becoming not just Gene Hill but man in the landscape. Kin and kindred.

It was natural that he thought of Katharine at times like these. At first she came to mind most readily when he focused on familiar details, such as the wild rose bushes, the cedar trees, or the chokecherry trees. These things he associated with his image of her. Then he moved beyond to other details, details native to the mountains and, deeper than that, native to the earth. One afternoon, lost in the trance of sun and water and rock and distant love, he sat on the shoal of a creek and watched a marmot on a rocky cliff across a pool from where he sat. The marmot worked its way back and forth from den to clifftop, along a ledge lined with scrub and stunted vines. Here he had it all — animal, plant, mineral, water, and sun — and he could feel Katharine's presence in all of it, just as he could feel her in the soapweed and sagebrush of the prairie. The spirit of the earth, which ran so strong in her and called to him, brought her to this place. It was a strong feeling, to have her wafted across the miles. It was as if they merged in the marmot and rock cliff, yet sat side by side in the timeless summer afternoon.

After that, he became more conscious of the focusing. He would see a detail, a thing, that spoke to him of her. It would become their apex, the point to which they both gravitated to merge. Sometimes it was a wild iris shoot or a low-lying clump of Oregon grape; sometimes it was an eagle flying in the crack of blue sky above the canyon where he watered his horse. When he was on ground high enough to watch the sunset, it was the sun; on clear nights it was the moon.

Once, while walking his horse along a hot shaly trail several hundred feet above the creek that ran past the marmot's home, he heard and then saw a rattler in his path. He did not merge with the snake, and he did not yearn to embrace it. Rather, he took a ten-pound rock and mashed its head and then kicked it twirling into the canyon. He laughed. He might be lunatic in love, but he wasn't hearing choo-choo trains yet.

On another day he again saw a scene that kept him inside himself. He was on foot, having left his horse tied and having come down a loose slope on foot, to get a drink of water and to see if a trail led out of there. It did.

The canyon was in shade this time of day — late morning — and the scene was slate gray. The shaly walls were gray, the flat boulders were gray, the sandbars were gray, and the pools of water were gray, reflecting the rocks and walls.

He knelt by a pool to drink cool clear water, his knees pushing in the soft moist sand. He set his hat on the sand next to him. He drank, and as he drank he had an awareness of being defenseless — his horse and rifle so far away as to be useless, his back to the world, even his head hatless. In that moment he trusted the world he drank from, and he knew such trust could be fatal.

He walked downstream to make sure of the trail before he brought the horse down. As he stepped onto a flat boulder that jutted into the creek, he saw a sight that made him freeze. He saw the head of a deer, a mule deer, with a set of forked horn antlers in velvet — a young buck, but no fawn or yearling. In a pool of water lay gobs of pale meat; chunks of hair floated on the surface. Back on the sandbar were other scattered tufts of hair but no other meat scraps, just piles of bear scat richly woven with deer hair. The attack had obviously taken place several days before, but the coarse sand was still worked up where the struggle had taken place. The prime young buck had probably been taking a drink.

He did not go out of himself into the scene, and he did not think of Katharine. He saw bloated scraps of dead meat, and he thought of Chet Bickford.

CHAPTER 13

The days flowed and halted and then streamed on. The brothers had been on the mountain nearly a month when they had their first visitor — human visitor, that is, for they had had their fair share of chipmunks, gray-jay camp robbers, and even a friendly raccoon.

Their visitor was Rusty George, welcome at any time but all the more welcome now, with two packhorses of grub and supplies. The three men spent the night at the base camp, where Rusty had unloaded the horses prior to finding the brothers.

As Gene and Zeke unpacked the goods, Rusty George expressed his surprise. "Well, by damn," he said, "Happy never packed such pretty things for me when I was out at camp. Looka there — canned peaches, dried apples, and damn if he didn't send you a can of them peppers."

"Told you to kiss the cook," Zeke said.

Then Gene found what he was hoping for — an envelope.

"What's that?" Rusty asked.

"Looks like Happy sent me a letter," Gene said.

"Go ahead and read it," Zeke said. "Me 'n'

Rusty can put away this grub and get somethin' cookin'.'"

Gene put the letter in his shirt pocket.

"Go read your mail," Zeke insisted. "We'll get the grub goin'."

"Oh, okay," Gene said. He went over to his bunk, lit a candle, and sat on the edge of the bunk to see what the mail held.

Happy's envelope had his letter as well as a small envelope with a letter in it. Gene had never seen Katharine's handwriting, but he knew it was hers when he saw his name written on the envelope.

The letter from Happy was short and conversational. It mentioned the weather, the day-to-day routine, and the hiring of two more hands to put up hay. Then there was a paragraph on Chet Bickford:

> Our friend Chet is still in the neighborhood. He says he is going to hire on with one of the outfits around here, but so far he is merely hanging on. He seems to be free with his opinion that you boys did in his brother. I understand he questioned Pete and Rusty rather closely that afternoon he was here, and I gather he asked some detailed questions about the time of day you boys got back from the ordeal with Bad Oscar. He is sure to cause more trouble. Be careful.

For the first time it occurred to Gene that he and Zeke were sent to the mountain not necessarily

155

to stay out of trouble, but to take trouble away from the ranch. Monte had not treated Gene like a troublemaker before, so this angle was unexpected. But it made sense. Monte was more or less washing his hands of the Hill brothers until they settled their differences with the Bickfords. With that realization came a new kind of loneliness, the feeling of having lost an important measure of trust.

He turned to Katharine's letter, hoping to be cheered. As he opened it he noticed it was written in a neat, close hand on a single page, and he saw at once that it was signed with love. He read the letter closely, slowly.

Dearest Gene:

Your letter came as a surprise but I was happy you found the time to write it. Tommy Tipton delivered it as you asked. He will also carry this letter back to Happy, who will keep it until it goes your way.

The sheriff was here right after you left last time. He said he was looking into Charlie's death. He wondered what the weather had been like on that day and I told him — a light steady rain. He asked if I knew anything else about Charlie or what he had been doing up until the time he died. I said no, I didn't look for knowledge about Charlie and all I knew was what I saw close by.

About a week after that, Charlie's brother

Chet came here. He asked the same kinds of questions. He is very much like Charlie, as you know, and if anything he makes me feel even more uncomfortable. I have seen him just the once.

On the lighter side, our friend Rusty George has been by. He seems to think I should be interested in him. He asked me right out if I'd slapped a brand on you or vice versa, which I think he meant had we declared anything. I said no and he seemed to think that meant an invitation to hang around and pester me with questions of what I liked to cook and cooked best. I don't think he means any harm and he has had nothing but good comments about you and Zeke both.

My mother and father are both doing fine. They understand I am waiting for you. So does Molly. I tell her how much I miss you. I wish I could just saddle her up and ride up to your mountain to see you, but I know we must wait for a while and I accept that. Sometimes at night I look up at the moon and know it is shining down on you wherever you are.

Take care of yourself, Gene. I hope for your safety every day, and I wait for the day you will be back.

Love,
Katharine

Gene stared blankly at the neatly written page. Both letters were warning him in some way about Chet. He looked over at Zeke, trimming up venison steaks. Chet was after them both, and it was not all Zeke's fault. Gene knew it was his own doing as well. They were in this mess together.

Then, on the brighter side, he looked at Rusty George, who was peeling onions to fry up with potatoes in the large black skillet. He smiled to think how Rusty had unwittingly carried the report of his own misdemeanor. No, Katharine was right. He meant no harm.

Gene put away his mail and then sat on the bench across from Rusty. "You'd make somebody a nice little wife someday, Rusty."

The cowpuncher wiped his knife on his shirt sleeve to remove a small wrinkled layer of onion membrane, and then he said, "Can't say as that's my first ambition, honey, but thanks for the offer."

"I wasn't thinkin' of myself," Gene bantered. "I'm not that selfish. I was thinkin' of those mail-order bulletins you've been known to receive, and how one of these days you'll write away and order one of them angels, and bring her out here to a sweet little honeymoon cabin like this, an' fetch water for her, and peel onions for her —"

"And rock the baby for her," said Zeke.

"You bet," teased Gene. "Once you teach her how to go out and check cows in a blizzard, you'll have it made."

Rusty stuck his knife in the table and gathered up the onion peels. "You wait," he said, going to the cabin door and throwing the peelings outside. "I'll give us a year, all three of us, and we'll see who has a blushing bride at the end of a year's time."

"I'll leave that bet to you two," Zeke said. "I'm in no hurry."

"Seems to me you like women well enough," Rusty said.

"I do. But it's the blushing bride part, and then the pup on the floor after that, in no time."

"Yes-sir," said Rusty, very gravely, "first one can come any time, they say. Yes-sir, Zeke. Be careful. First comes love, then comes marriage, then comes Zeke with a baby carriage."

"I'm careful," Zeke avowed.

"Not that you ever minded the first part," Rusty went on. "Puttin' the bun in the oven to begin with."

"I told you I'm careful."

"Well, then, warmin' the oven."

They all three laughed and took up their work again. Rusty George cut up the onions, Gene peeled the potatoes, and Zeke trimmed away the tough rind that had formed on the venison while it hung curing. It was a jolly bachelor outfit, and soon they had the two skillets slicked with bacon grease and spluttering with the evening's supper.

When supper was on the table, Gene set the dishpan of water on the cookstove. Zeke and Rusty were already digging in when he sat down. It was good hot food, welcome food for hungry men at the end of a long day. No one said much until all the food was gone.

"Good grub," said Rusty. "Who gets to do the pearl divin'?"

"I'll take care of it," Gene said, rising and gathering the wrecks. "You're the guest of honor."

"Suit yourself," said Rusty. "I've washed dishes before and I reckon I'll get a chance to wash 'em again sometime."

"For the little woman," Zeke said dryly as he fished for the tobacco sack in his shirt pocket.

"Maybe," said Rusty George. "And maybe again I'll just find me a first-class pearl diver." He pried a toothpick into his lower teeth and looked at Zeke.

Zeke rolled his cigarette, licked it and tapped it, and lit it. "I hope you do. Then me 'n' Gene can come bummin' around about suppertime."

Rusty smiled at Gene. "Oh, I bet Gene'll be all fixed up for himself not too long after that."

Gene smiled and nodded as he shook soap flakes into the dishwater. Yes, the cabin on down the trail was still there, and there was a dark-haired pretty girl in the doorway.

A few days after Rusty George's visit, the boys had their second and less welcome visitor. It was Chet himself. He showed up at suppertime, as anyone might, but Gene had the feeling that Chet had not gotten there that very moment. The horse did not seem tired and the sweat was dry around the saddle blanket; Gene could see that much in the twilight. Chet himself seemed casual and well-rested, and he put on the air of friendliness that

Charlie had assumed for short periods of time.

Gene did not like having Chet there, not at all. They all three knew he was not welcome on Redboot, and this was a Redboot cow camp. Nevertheless, there was no open admission that Chet had a reason to be their enemy, and to turn another rider away from supper and a night's lodging was simply not done. And so, despite his deepest distrust, Gene invited Chet to eat and to spend the night. Chet, acting as if he had never spoken a single word of disparagement in any of the saloons or bunkhouses in the country, accepted.

Zeke fried bacon and the last of their potatoes while Gene sat at the table. Chet, who was chewing tobacco, stood leaning against the wall and occasionally went to the cabin door to spit outside. In between spits he let it be known that he was going to hire on with one of the outfits down below, hadn't decided which one yet, but in the meanwhile was taking a little time to hunt mountain lions.

"Poor time of year to hunt wildcats, I'd think," Zeke said.

"Then you don't have to go along," Chet snapped back.

"Your business," Zeke conceded.

"I'd think so."

Gene was troubled by the unlikely story and by the puzzle of why Chet had come so openly. Was he there to pick a fight with both of them? Was he there to antagonize and intimidate? Or was he there to murder them in their sleep? In any case, Gene certainly didn't trust Chet, and he planned not to have both their backs turned on him at the same time. So Zeke cooked, and Gene would wash the dishes.

After a wordless and largely joyless supper, Gene cleared the table as the other two rolled cigarettes.

"Well, Zeke," Chet began, "seems like your stay up here might keep you away from that yellow-haired gal."

"You must mean Jane." Zeke wasn't giving him much rope.

"I must."

Here it comes, Gene thought.

"Yeah, Zeke, you know, I knew her before you did. Before you or Charlie either one did." Chet paused, as if giving Zeke a chance to answer.

"I think I heard that somewhere."

Gene almost laughed.

"Yeah, I knew her pretty well. Pretty well."

"Is that right."

"Some things I could tell you about her, but they'd prob'ly never do you any good."

"Probably not."

"But I don't worry about her anymore."

"Uh-huh."

"Don't worry much about women, though I see a few of 'em here and there."

That's for me, Gene thought.

"I suppose," Zeke said, blowing out a cloud of smoke.

"What do you mean, you suppose?"

"If you say it, I suppose you mean it."

"You're not callin' me a liar, then."

"No reason to. You say you know a lot of women here and there. That's your business."

"I suppose," Chet said with evident mockery. "I'll tell you what I've found out about 'em. Women are whores. You know that? They're whores, all of 'em, in one way or another."

"One man's opinion," Gene said. He could feel his blood rising, and he took warning.

"What'd you say?"

"One man's opinion," Gene said clearly.

"That's right. One man's opinion. That's all." Chet pushed himself up from the table and walked to the door, where he hawked and spit.

Gene noticed two things when Chet's back was turned. He was not wearing his spurs, which confirmed Gene's suspicion that he might have been moving around quietly in the earlier part of the day. Also, his bootheels were worn on the outsides, just as Charlie's had been.

When Chet turned around and walked back toward the table, he made an unconscious gesture that Gene had seen Charlie make a thousand times. He put the first and second fingers of his right hand to his crotch and pulled lightly upward, as if to adjust himself. Gene had seen the move in Charlie whenever he was swaggering or assuming an air of dominance. That seemed to be what Chet was up to, standing and looming while Zeke sat, as Gene had done earlier. Yes, that was it. Rather than sit back down at the table, Chet returned to leaning against the wall. That was what he was here for, to be king coyote.

"Just one man's opinion," he resumed, still pushing.

Neither Gene nor Zeke said anything.

"Probably not somethin' a couple of boys like you want to hear, way up here so far away from your gal friends."

"We get by," Gene said.

"I suppose," Chet mocked. "But it's an old saying. Did you know that, Zeke?"

"If you say so."

"Not because I say so. I just heard it. And learned it. Goes along with another saying, you know, Zeke?"

"Which one is that?"

"The one that says every child knows its own mother, but it's a smart child knows who its father is."

"I think I heard that somewhere."

"I suppose." Chet turned to Gene. "What do you think, Gene?"

Gene wondered what he was getting at. Was there some veiled insult in Katharine's direction, about either her virtue or her parents? It didn't seem like it, but it was clear that Chet was trying to taunt both brothers. "I don't know, Chet. Sounds like ancient wisdom."

"Like I said, I just learned it, that's all."

Gene decided to change the subject. "What would we think about some coffee? Stove's still hot, and I could make some."

Zeke yawned. "Sure. It won't keep me awake."

"I'd go for some," Chet said. "I've got a ways to go yet tonight."

Gene realized Chet had not brought in any gear earlier. He was glad Chet wasn't staying, but he said, "You're welcome to bunk here, you know."

"Thanks all the same, but I want to be up on top to track that cat in the morning."

"Suit yourself," Zeke said, in a neat echo of Rusty George.

"I will."

In less than an hour they had had their coffee and Chet was gone. As the hoofbeats thumped away in the night, Gene and Zeke looked at each other.

"What do you think?" Gene asked.

"Some kind of mountain lion hunter." With his tongue, Zeke pushed a toothpick through the gap between his teeth.

"He'll be around here bird-doggin' us till he can get us to fight."

Zeke nodded.

"He wants both of us," Gene said. "That's how he wants to square things."

"In a pig's ass," Zeke said. "He's not goin' to get anybody. If that cat hunter gets anything, he'll get hurt, that's all."

CHAPTER 14

From the time of Chet's visit onward, there was no being at ease on the mountain. Both Gene and Zeke knew there was the constant threat of attack. They knew they were vulnerable at night as they sat around the campfire or in the lantern-lit tent. When they were at the cabin they felt a little bit safer, but a bold man could take them on there too, as it seemed Chet might have done the evening he ate with them. Danger might come to them as they slept, also, but as Gene reasoned it from a killer's point of view, there would be a greater chance of botching the job that way. In the broad light of day Gene felt the most vulnerable, always as if there might be a rifle sight covering his shoulder blades. Zeke admitted to the same queasy feeling, never knowing if he was watched.

At first they thought they should ride together whenever possible, under the idea that in union there is strength. At night in a closed area that was probably the case, but in talking it over they decided to stay apart in open daylight. If Chet indeed wanted to get them, as it seemed he did, he would do it easiest if he rimrocked them at the same time. It was not a pleasant thought to consider, but they brought it out in the open and considered their chances. If Chet got to one of them while he was by himself, it might take days or even longer to get at the other, who in the meantime might get even or get away and reach help. So Chet's odds were best in broad daylight when they were together.

Chet had one clear advantage, as they saw it. It was a one-way feud. They could not go out and hunt Chet down. They had no justification. But he could stalk them, justified by his certainty.

"It's too bad the whole thing isn't out in the open," Gene said one evening as they sat by a dying campfire.

"No doubt about that at this point," Zeke agreed. "But I just can't picture saying, 'Here it is, Chet. I killed your brother in a fair fight. And then Gene helped me cover it up because we got rattled. Let's you and me settle it.' "

"No, we couldn't. He's convinced we doubled up on Charlie and would do the same on him, so it works to his advantage if things stay the way they are. He thinks he has to deal with both of us no matter what, so he'll pick the time."

"And meanwhile wear us down with fret and worry."

"That's for sure."

"And besides," Zeke said, "even if we did 'fess up now, which would only get you in some needless trouble, it wouldn't cool him off. As soon as the law was done with us, he'd be right back like he is now."

Gene nodded. He felt the cold, dark world of the mountain all around them.

"And he's right about one thing, I think," Zeke said.

"What's that?"

"About us teaming up. What would you do if he killed me?"

"I'd go after him, I guess," Gene replied.

"So would I. And if he was gettin' the best of me and not lettin' up?"

"Sooner or later I'd have to step in."

"Me too. So he's right, in that respect."

Gene laughed halfway. "Yeah. He wouldn't have a chance at this point unless he was losin'."

"So he picks his time."

"And wears us down with fret and worry."

Zeke threw his cigarette stub into the campfire coals. "That's the only damn reason I wish the business about Charlie was out in the open. We could hunt him right back."

Gene laughed and shook his head. "No, we couldn't, unless we wanted another body to dispose of."

Zeke flashed a malicious grin. "We'd do a better job of it the second time."

Gene let out a weary sigh. He was in it to the end with his brother, like it had been when they were boys. Back then, he had felt that he and Zeke were one, joined and inseparable. But now that they were men, he and Zeke stood apart as two separate, almost unrelated people. He would stick with his brother, but he wished Zeke were less wild and showed more conscience.

So the fret and worry wore on, from one day to the next, for over three weeks. The boys figured it was near time for another load of supplies, and they expected to see Rusty George any day now. They were at the cabin again for a few days.

"We could certainly use the grub," Zeke said one night at supper, "and you've just about wore out that one love letter."

"I wouldn't object to a little more readin' material."

"You probably have somethin' to send by return mail, too."

"I might have an envelope for our messenger boy."

In truth, Gene had written four letters to Katharine, all of them short and all of them now in the same envelope. Each time he wrote, he had the urge to make a clean breast of his part in Charlie's death. It pained him to keep it hidden from her, especially now that he imagined the possibility of not living to see her again. The desire for confession was strong in him, but to protect both Zeke and himself, he chose not to put down anything that could become evidence of their guilt.

"Well, it'll be nice to see someone from down below," Zeke said, "and Rusty George would be a welcome sight."

Company did come the very next day. Gene, who was alert every second for any sign of human activity, saw two riders approach from the far end of a meadow. He eased his horse into the timber and watched the riders come nearer. Suddenly he recognized the bay Pepper and the dun mare Molly, bearing light-haired Happy and dark-haired Katharine. Gene felt a rush of joy as he put his horse into a lope across the meadow. She waved as she recognized him. He felt the familiar flutter in his stomach, and he waved back. What a beautiful woman! And what a good friend Happy was, to come all this way himself and to chaperone the prairie princess, as he called her.

"Howdy, stranger," she said, as he drew his horse up next to hers. "Be still, Molly."

"Howdy," he said, taking her hand. "Happy," he said, "what do you think of the eagle's nest up on the cliff there?"

As Happy turned to look at the cliff, Gene closed in for the kiss. "I'm not sure that I can see an eagle's . . . oh, I'm sorry." He looked away again.

Gene and Katharine laughed together. "Sorry, Happy," Gene said, "but it's been two months, almost."

"Quite all right," Happy said smiling, "but you had my hopes up, you scamp. Now you owe it to me to show me an eagle's nest."

Gene looked at the sun and squinted in thought. "I know where there's one not too much out of our way. We need to go tell Zeke you're here, and we can make a little detour and still get back to the cabin before dark."

"Lead the way," said Happy.

Gene and Katharine rode stirrup to stirrup in the broad sunlight, and the world again seemed full of promise. The lush meadow, the fragrant pines, the towering mountainsides, and the clear blue sky — this was the way life was supposed to be, wide and open and free. The thought of Chet Bickford flashed through his mind but briefly; he knew Chet wouldn't make a move while visitors were here. Then he was joyful again, in the company of his beautiful woman and the true friend who had brought her here.

They paused to admire the eagle's nest, across a gully and up a sheer cliff, a clinging structure of twigs and sticks, safe and majestic and out of reach. No eagles were visible at the moment, but the character of the nest gave a sense of the eagle's power and solitude.

When they had gazed enough, they headed north along the edge of a meadow, where the afternoon shadows were beginning to stretch. Suddenly a rifle shot broke the afternoon stillness ahead of them. Gene looked at Katharine and then at Happy. "That's where Zeke is," he said, stopping his horse.

"We'd better get over there, then," Happy said.

"If it's trouble," Katharine said, "he needs us."

Gene hesitated, grinding his teeth and waiting to hear a second shot. None came. "Okay," he said. "Let's string out. I'll go first."

He led the way along the meadow's edge and then into a stand of timber, following a cow trail uphill, then down into a draw, and up again. Gene slowed his horse to a walk, then stopped at the edge of the next meadow. He studied the meadow, seeing where the cattle had bunched up at the far end. Next he saw Bucky at the edge of the timber, cropping grass. Then he felt a wave of relief as he saw Zeke, apparently working on something on the ground. Gene exhaled a long breath as he turned to Katharine.

"Looks like he's got some meat on the ground," he said, loud enough for her and Happy both.

She nodded and rode Molly up alongside him, and side by side again they rode, trotting along the edge of the meadow with Happy bringing up the rear guard.

Zeke had his hat off and his sleeves rolled up, and his hands were bloody. He straightened up and looked at the approaching riders. He waved with the hand that held the knife.

As Gene brought his horse to a halt he saw that Zeke had killed a fat spike bull elk. "Had me scared for a minute there, Zeke. I didn't know you were hunting today."

"Me neither, but I saw this young elk and decided not to pass it up. Looks like you brought Happy for protection."

"And Katharine. Zeke, this is Katharine Rose. Katharine, this is my brother Zeke, red-handed as you can see."

Katharine laughed. "I'm pleased to meet you, Zeke."

"Equally pleased," he said, and then nodding at her right hand, which held the reins, he teased, "You rope left-handed?"

"Not much." She put both hands on the pommel, shook her head, and smiled.

Zeke's eyes flashed beneath his widow's peak, and the gap in his teeth showed as he smiled. "Just wonderin'."

"Good job for you," she teased back.

"I suppose," he said, and then, looking at Happy, he said, "hello to you, Happy."

"Hello, Zeke." Happy rode up to look at the spike bull. "That's a nice one. Did you know we were coming?"

"I'd like to say yes, but . . ."

"Just lucky, I guess."

Zeke laughed. "Yeah, just lucky. You and me both."

Happy gave him a questioning look.

"We can send some of this home with you," Zeke explained.

"I'd certainly take some of it."

"We'll hang it in quarters tonight, and it'll be cool enough to make the ride back."

Happy nodded. "How do we get it back to camp?"

"Now that I got help," Zeke said, "I'll bet we can quarter it and haul back a quarter each." He looked around. "How about it?"

Gene and Happy nodded. The three men looked at Katharine, who said, "I think Molly can carry two quarters, and I can ride with someone else."

Gene's eyes met hers, and it was if he went out of himself just that quickly. Then he looked at his brother.

Zeke grinned. "Looks like you got yourself a passenger, Gene."

Katharine wrinkled her nose, her eyes still sparkling. "I'd rather do it that way than carry a quarter of an animal in my lap."

With Gene and Happy holding the animal by its legs and rolling it this way and that, Zeke skinned the front half on the ground. Then he cut off the hocks and the head. He found a rock and was beginning to use it as a hammer on the back of his knife, to cut through the pelvis, when Happy brought out a small hatchet from his saddlebags.

"Came prepared, huh?" Zeke said. "Thanks."

"My traveling kit," Happy answered.

Zeke split the pelvis with quick forceful strokes, then he loosened the last four ribs on each side of the backbone. With his knife he separated the animal's front half from the back, leaving it attached only by the spine, which he severed with a few swift strokes of the hatchet. Happy and Gene dragged the hind quarters aside and left them splayed out, fresh side upward, to cool.

"That went quick," Zeke said. "I thought I was goin' to have to do it all with my knife."

Now he rolled the front half so he could cut away the backstrap, or loin, from the backbone on one side. Having done that, he used the hatchet to separate the ribs from the spine on that side, so that the front half lay in two quarters. Finished, he straightened his back for a rest.

Gene, who had appreciated Zeke's dexterity

through the whole process, said, "You do good work, Zeke. Nice head shot like that, and there's no bloody mess or bloodshot meat."

Zeke beamed. Then he went to the elk's head and pulled the corner of its mouth into a grin, exposing the ivory tooth. Zeke worked his knife point in and pried out the ivory. Then he flipped the head over and got out the other tooth. He held them in his hand to show Katharine, and then he put them in his pocket, saying, "Good luck."

"Don't forget the tongue," said Gene.

Zeke was a picture with his hat off, his wild black hair loose, his shirt sleeves rolled up, and his hands and forearms vermilion with dried blood as he offered the knife to Gene.

"Go ahead," Gene said. "You're doin' fine. No sense in both of us getting all messy."

Zeke flipped the knife so that it did a half-turn in the air and the handle settled into his palm. Then he pivoted and turned and leaned, and with a few slashes on the underside of the elk's jaws and then a couple of jabs down its throat, he drew out the limp tongue. He tossed it onto one of the fresh front quarters.

"And the heart and liver," said Happy.

Zeke shrugged and stepped over to the gut pile, where he trimmed out Happy's request. "Anything else?" he asked, his good nature clearly still on top.

"Maybe a violin and a bottle of vintage red wine," said Happy.

"As soon as we get back to the palace," Zeke answered back.

They loaded the hind quarters onto Molly, hair side down in one attached piece, with the saddle horn sticking through a slash in the hide. Zeke tied the load down and lashed it across, tight. Happy repacked his saddlebags to make room for the organ meat and then got mounted. Zeke handed him a front quarter. Then Zeke was up on Bucky, and Gene hoisted the last quarter up to him.

Gene stepped up onto Dodger, then kicked his stirrup free for Katharine. She put her foot in and took a hand up. Gene looked over his left shoulder for a quick kiss, and then, with her arms around his waist, he handed Molly's reins to her. They fell into line, following two horses and leading one. Zeke was in the lead carrying an eighty-pound triangle of fresh meat in his lap, and singing "Oh Susanna."

There was no violin or bottle of vintage wine at the palace after all, but the foursome had a merry supper anyway. Happy and Katharine cooked while the boys took care of the stock and hung out the meat. Happy had brought carrots and greens from his garden, so they had an uncommon meal for a cow camp in the mountains.

After supper, Zeke and Happy offered to wash the dishes. Zeke, who seemed to enjoy putting his brother on the spot, said casually, "You two prob'ly have some stargazin' to catch up on."

Once outside, Gene said to Katharine, "I've read your letter just about every day since I got it. I look at the moon every night."

Her hand found his as she said, "So do I. It brings us together when we're apart, doesn't it?"

They met in a kiss, a long kiss. When they separated he held her at arm's length in the moonlight. "You look so wonderful," he said.

Her eyes sparkled as she said, "You look pretty good yourself."

Then they moved into a close embrace, cheek to cheek, as he told her for the first time, "I love you, Katharine."

And the soft voice whispered back, "I love you, Gene."

They walked and they talked and they stopped and then walked on. Eventually they found a place to sit, where they could see the broad starry sky above and the one illumined window of the cabin across the meadow.

"I have something to tell you," he said at last.

"Go ahead." She squeezed his hand.

"It's something I kept from you before, but I think I should tell you now."

She squeezed his hand again.

"It's something I'm not proud of, but it's something you should know if we think we should be — partners. Or if something should happen to me."

"It's bad, isn't it, Gene?"

"Yes, it is."

"Then you had better tell me." She kissed him

on the cheek. "It will be better for both of us."

Here it goes, he thought. "It's about Charlie. He didn't die the way it seems. He died in a fight. With Zeke. Zeke killed him. I was there, and if it means anything, it was a fair fight. And then I helped him make it seem like Charlie died out on the range by himself."

"Then his brother Chet and Sheriff Rolfe aren't just dreaming things up."

"No, they aren't, but they've gone as far as they can go with it, and there's really no way we can go back and clear things up."

Then he told her the story in more detail, beginning with Bad Oscar and how things had gone wrong there, and then the fight and the storm. More briefly he told of the sheriff's visit and Chet's, followed by Chet's odd visit to the mountain. "So it seems to me, at least, and to Zeke, that there's not much we can do to change things. We just have to wait for him to make a move, if he's ever goin' to."

"He scares me, Gene."

"He's a threat, that's for sure." He took a deep breath. "Anyway, I wanted to tell you all this, in person, so you'd understand."

"I think I understand. And I love you all the more for telling me."

"Then we're still partners?"

"Of course we're still partners." She turned her face to him in the moonlight, and he saw her dark hair and sparkling clear eyes. Then they both closed their eyes as their lips met.

A few minutes later he spoke. "You know, a couple of months ago I told myself there was no such thing as a secret in this country. Then I got drawn into this tangle and tried to keep it secret, but it just won't stay hidden, not the way Chet spreads it around." He kissed her on the cheek. "And you know, it hasn't seemed right, trying to keep a secret from you."

"You didn't. Not for long. And now everything is right."

"Yes it is, isn't it."

"Yes it is. Everything is right."

Their lips met again, and it seemed as if they had suddenly walked hand-in-hand into the sunlight.

Back at the cabin, there was a pot of coffee ready. Gene set out cups as Happy poured the coffee. Gene sensed an air of confidence between his brother and the cook, and he asked Zeke, "Did you tell Happy about our most recent visitor?"

"I mentioned it."

Happy nodded.

"That's good," Gene said. "No secrets in this camp. That makes all four of us up to date."

Katharine smiled at Zeke, a smile that said, "You are my partner's brother. I accept you."

Zeke smiled back, a smile that seemed to convey an emotion that Gene did not often see displayed in his brother. It seemed like gratitude.

Zeke's rare moment passed, however, and he resumed his festive mood from the afternoon. "Let's sing," he said. "Let's sing a couple of songs before we call it a night."

They sang "My Darling Clementine," "Oh, Susanna!," "Sweet Betsy from Pike," and "Git Along, Little Dogies." Then Katharine suggested a religious song, since it was Sunday. After some discussion they settled on "Softly and Tenderly." Katharine and Happy made a good duet, while Gene and Zeke sang along with the words they knew and hummed the rest.

As the group of four joined in the soothing hymn, Gene wondered what it would be like to be outside the cabin at a time like this, hearing the gentle invitation for sinners to come home.

CHAPTER 15

The men slept out under the moon and stars that night, leaving the cabin to Katharine. She protested the extravagance, but Gene told her it was a small thing. It was a warm, clear night, and for all she knew, maybe Zeke or Happy snored and was shy about it. He assured her that if it were winter, they wouldn't be so gallant.

It was really not that warm outside, and Gene was glad to have the canvas that worked as ground sheet and cover to his soogans. He lay on his back and looked at the moon. Zeke went to sleep immediately and was soon snoring; not too long later, Happy was also asleep, letting out an occasional snuffle snore. Gene smiled. He had been told he snored, too, but he was sure Katharine would get used to it. If it was true.

As he looked at the moon he thought of her, especially of her expressive face in the moonlight, shining with love and concern. He was thankful she hadn't blamed Zeke for the present danger. Some women would, as he imagined Virginia might. Some women might even try to persuade him, at this point, to break with his brother in whatever way he might. But Katharine knew in-

181

tuitively how he felt, and she went with it. She was an only child, but it seemed to Gene that she saw the brother bond and understood it.

Brotherhood was a strong tie. For all of the crudeness and bad temper of the Bickfords, they were brothers too, first and last. Zeke had broken their brother bond, and in Chet's mind, Gene had broken it too.

Gene feared Chet and at some level probably disliked him nearly to the point of hatred, but he could not blame Chet for his blood hatred against Zeke and himself. Chet was ugly in his nature and he had a kill-or-be-killed attitude in his current vendetta, but his having had and lost a brother made him human.

Somewhere Chet was probably sleeping, and far away his brother was buried. Gene listened to Zeke snoring. Here they were, sleeping side by side as they had done all their lives, and in another day or week, one or both of them might be dead. It was a difficult idea to comprehend.

Thoughts of his own mortality often came to Gene when he was on his way to sleep. He had learned that such thoughts usually led nowhere and were just as well brushed aside. So he turned his thoughts to a happier image, the glow of a soft expressive face in the moonlight — the woman he loved, who was now sleeping in the nearby cabin under the same moon.

Happy and Katharine prepared to leave shortly after sunrise the next morning, with half an elk on the packhorses.

Gene held her stirrup out for her, but she was in no hurry to put her foot into it. "I'll miss you," she said.

"And I'll miss you. I hope it's not another two months."

"I'll try to come again."

"If you can," he said. "The old man might keep me here till the snow flies."

Tears began to start in her eyes, and he dropped the stirrup and took her in his arms.

"Be careful, Gene."

"I will. Let's both be brave. And I'll see you before long."

He felt her wet eyelashes against his face as he kissed her. Then he held her stirrup, and like a brave girl she was on board Molly and quick-stepping to join Happy. She turned in the saddle and waved. He waved back. Then she rode off into the mountain morning.

As Gene and Zeke saddled their horses in the dark stable, Zeke said, "Not to make you worry, but I got this feelin' that somethin's goin' to happen before long."

"I know what you mean. If Chet's been watchin', which I imagine he has, he knows we have company about once a month, and our company just left."

"Kinda what I was thinkin'."

"Zeke?"

"Yeah?"

"I can't help thinkin' what a lousy thing it was to leave Charlie out in the rain like that."

Zeke looked at him as if he had said something embarrassing. "Well, I guess it was. But what can we do about it now?"

"Just try to keep from gettin' killed, I guess."

Zeke leaned his left elbow against his saddled horse and pushed his hat back. "Gene," he said, "you'd better get your mind right about this. There's a man out there wants to see us both dead, and he's about ready to make his move. We can't let it happen if we can help it."

"What can we do, then?"

"Try to get him first."

"I don't think I could do that, Zeke."

Zeke had gone cold. "You might not get to." Then he led his horse out of the barn and into the morning sun.

As Gene pulled his latigo, he wondered what Zeke meant. Did he mean he, Zeke, would get to Chet first? Or did he mean Chet would get to Gene before Gene had a fighting chance? Gene shrugged. Then he tucked the loose end of the latigo and led his horse into the sunlight. He let Zeke get a quarter mile ahead of him, as they had agreed to do, and then he turned out for another day's work.

Early that afternoon the sky started clouding over. They had decided the day before that today they would bunch the herd so the next day they could move it to better grazing. So they spent the morning bringing cattle, two or three pairs at a time, to the large meadow where Gene had met their visitors the day before. Gene, who never completely forgot about Chet, was nevertheless able to keep his mind on his work. Now, as the clouds began to gather on the peaks, his thoughts ran mainly to the dangers of slick trails, scattering cattle, and lightning on high ground. He was pushing along a fat cow and her bounding calf when he felt a sting on his left ribs and his horse start plunging, and then he heard the booming crash of the rifle.

It was here and now! The juice of fear raced through him in a split second as Dodger pitched, blood welling out of the neck just ahead of the saddle. He knew several things at once. Chet was behind him. The horse was hit and might go down. If the horse sulled he would be a sitting duck.

He raked the horse with his spurs as he shucked the rifle. Cattle were stampeding to the far end of the pasture and crashing into the timber, and Dodger was grunting and heaving. It would be hard for Chet to draw down fine on him. Gene kicked loose his stirrups and the horse blew him off. He hit the ground on his feet, stumbled, and then zigzagged for the nearest timber. A bullet split the air above his head, and he ducked to run in a crouch. The shot crashed, and then after a pause came a third shot. Glancing back, he saw Dodger go down in the hindquarters. Then Gene was at the edge of the timber, and as the fourth shot whined and boomed he pitched headlong into the cover.

His mouth was dry and his heart was pounding, but he had his wits about him. Chet must be up and to the right, on the rim where Happy had looked in vain for the eagle's nest. Dodger was on the ground and trying to get up, pulling with his front hooves and squealing. Suddenly the horse's head snapped over, and another shot shattered the air. Gene licked his lips and swallowed hard. He was alive, bleeding on the left side but not hurt bad. Glancing at the rimrock, he knew Chet must be furious. He had botched his first shot, not by much and closer than he probably knew, but bungled all the same. So he took it out on the horse.

Zeke of course had heard and would be on his way, cautiously. Please, Zeke, thought Gene, be quiet just this once.

Gene felt the gash on his rib as he looked at the dead horse, blood glistening in the gray daylight. This was real. It was out in the open now, no more cat and mouse. It was kill or be killed, both ways.

He tried to place Chet, but there was no direct sunlight to give a glint to a rifle barrel. He imagined how the bullet had traveled to nick his ribs and to hit Dodger's neck the way it did, and he tried to determine the place and the angle at which they would have been riding. Yes, that would put the man in the spot where Gene had imagined him a few minutes earlier.

Still there was no sign of Zeke. Gene decided he would have to make sure where Chet was, then he would keep a close eye on him. If he didn't, Chet could sneak down and around on him and shoot him like a skunk in the barnyard.

He levered a shell into his rifle, then got into a steady position, resting the rifle on his hand on a log. He decided to send four searching shots, about three feet apart, in the spot where he had Chet placed. When shots came back, he would have to place their source at the same time he dodged bullets.

Firing four quick shots and hoping he had his sniper distracted, he moved fifteen yards to his left, in a crouch. Then a hail of bullets, six of them, came crashing into the thicket he had fired from. Chet was apparently not worried about giving away his position, firing openly as he did. Now Gene saw him, or rather movement that must be him, pretty well in the spot Gene had figured.

Well enough, he thought. There was no point in throwing lead at this distance. Now it would be wait and see — wait to see what Chet would do next, and wait for Zeke to show up.

Gene looked at Dodger, fair meat for coyotes and buzzards. It had been pretty close. If Chet had made a better shot, Gene could be lying out there, eyes wide to the coming rain, also. It wasn't over yet, but he was sure of one thing: Chet had gotten his last shot at Gene Hill's back. It was an open fight now, and they had Chet two to one. Chet was no doubt confident he was still going to win, but Gene thought otherwise. It was kill or be killed. He knew he would kill Chet Bickford if he got him in his sights, and he would take care of consequences later. He looked at Dodger and then at the rimrock. Yes, he knew he could do it if it came up.

He heard tramping in the timber behind him, and he knew Chet hadn't had time to get around that soon. Nevertheless, he had his rifle at the ready until he made a positive identification of his brother.

"Gene!" It was a loud whisper.

"Over here."

Zeke came stepping over, lightly like a cat, and settled next to Gene. His face was ablaze with excitement.

Gene tossed his head in the direction of the dead horse.

Zeke saw and nodded. "He doesn't miss every time."

"His first shot was pretty close." Gene showed Zeke the torn shirt and the cut flesh, which had already quit bleeding its trickle.

Zeke nodded and looked at the horse again. "Well," he said, "this is sure it. We go after him, the son of a bitch. Where is he? Up there?"

Gene pointed. "I had him placed right there. Straight down from that group of three pines."

"Uh-huh." Zeke studied the layout. "We can get him if he stays put." He squinted a little longer and nodded again. "What do you think if we try it this way. You stay right here, maybe move around a little, and every ten minutes or so you fire a shot or two up there. As long as I hear his shots comin' back, I'll know where he is. How does that sound?"

"Easy enough for me."

"You still have to keep from getting killed."

"I intend to. Now, what's your plan for yourself?"

"I'm thinkin' I can work up and around back of him, and shoot him like a mountain goat."

"How long do you think it'll take?"

"About an hour, maybe a little more."

Their eyes met. "Okay, Zeke. I hope he's there when you get there."

There was malice in Zeke's smile. "I'll get him."

Gene held out his hand, and Zeke clasped it. Gene felt a lump in his throat as he said, "Good luck. And be careful."

Zeke winked and drew his finger across his throat.

Gene laughed and shook his head. He was on the thin line between laughing and crying. This might be the last time they saw each other alive, and here Zeke was, making it into a game. He thought, Zeke's got nerve. This is his way of not letting it get to him. Gene forced a smile. "Every ten minutes," he said.

Zeke smiled and winked again, obviously in encouragement, and then he was creeping away through the timber with his rifle. Gene watched him and thought what an amazing force life was, to be surging in a man like Zeke, and yet it could be cut short just like Dodger's. That's the way it had been with Charlie — raging with life one minute, and dead as a rock the next. Gene exhaled, long and low. He could wish it only one way. If anyone died, he hoped it was not his brother.

He thought of Katharine, just getting home by now, with no inkling of how soon the danger had come down. And he thought of that cabin a little ways down the trail, and he saw her there . . . That was the way it had to be. He imagined children — a baby in her arms, a larger child in his lap. He and Katharine as parents. Partners for life.

Gene checked his rifle. There was a live shell in the chamber. He squinted at the rimrock. An old cowpuncher he had worked with had once told him a man could see clearer if he squinted and strained. It never worked for Gene, but he found himself trying it anyway.

Zeke had not been gone ten minutes yet — maybe six or seven. He imagined the triangle formed by Chet, Zeke, and himself. Chet was the apex, and the angle was changing as Zeke moved on his arc, making a different triangle with each step.

Then, out of nowhere, filling the stillness of the afternoon not far away, came the terrifying report of a rifle. The shot died away and there were no other sounds. Gene felt icy all over. The shot had been fired where Zeke would have been. Had Chet come down while he and Zeke had been conferring, and ground-sluiced Zeke unawares? Zeke had been so cheerful and confident when he left, he would have taken a while to tune into the seriousness of the hunt.

Gene's mouth was dry. One shot and no more. No Zeke calling out. No return gunfire. Suddenly the world seemed emptied out, large and hollow and haunting. He was alone. The sun was gone. For a second he lost his sense of direction and the sense of whose eyes he was looking through. He shook his head and focused on the rimrock. That was west. He was Gene. Not far away his brother Zeke was either standing or not standing. This might be it, here in the gray-green pine and aspens of a cloudy day. There might be a man, dangerous and full of purpose, coming for him any minute. The breeze was cold. He was thirsty. There was no noise, only silence. He eased back the hammer on his rifle. He was ready.

Then he heard footfalls in the timber, coming his way. It was the tramp of a man, careless as an unspooked deer.

Then a voice. "Gene!"

"Over here."

"I got him. It's all clear now."

CHAPTER 16

Zeke's hands were shaking as he buttoned his pants back up from urinating. He was talking excitedly. "I can't believe it. He rode right up to me. Like a big buck deer. Not thirty yards away. Never saw me. I came around on him and blew him right out of the saddle." Zeke was exhilarated. "I just can't believe it. He came right to me. Bam! Just like that! I didn't even have time to think. I just reacted."

"You're sure you got him?"

"Oh, yeah." Zeke's eyes widened. "He's got a hole in him as big as my fist. You bet he's dead."

"You're sure?"

"Hell, yes, I'm sure. I stood right over him."

"I keep thinkin' he's up there." Gene jerked his head west.

"No, he's right over there. Go see for yourself."

"I believe you. Boy, I could use a drink of water."

Zeke looked in Dodger's direction. "I'll go get some."

Gene looked at the rimrock.

"Gene, he's dead. I killed the son of a bitch."

Zeke ran bouncing to the dead horse and came

back with the canteen. He was clearly elated. He took a long drink and handed the canteen to his brother. "It was unbelievable. Bam!" He snapped his fingers. "Just like that!"

Gene let the water hit bottom. He capped the canteen. Things were sinking in. "Let's think about how we're goin' to handle this one," he said.

"If there was a river close by, we could dam it up, change its course, bury him, and then run the water back over him." Zeke laughed.

"Come on, now," Gene said sternly. "We can't lie about it. Not this time."

"No," Zeke agreed. "This one's got a bullet hole. We'll have to hide the body."

Gene looked at him.

"Don't worry," Zeke said. "I'll take care of it. I'll bury him. You don't even have to see him. This is all my doing." Zeke seemed eager to take charge, to keep bounding on his wave of energy. A final surge seemed to come on him, and then he calmed down. He drew his lips tightly over his teeth and licked them. He nodded and said, "I'll take care of him."

Gene was unsure. He wanted to stay out of it if he could, but he didn't want to shove it off on his brother. "You shouldn't have to do it all, Zeke."

"Look, *I* killed him. *I'll* bury him. We'll leave you out of this one. You'll be in the clear."

Gene had a thought. "Where's his horse?"

"It took off."

"I didn't hear it."

Zeke pointed north. "It was off and gone that way 'fore he hit the ground." Then he frowned. "I'd like to find that horse and kill it. Horses don't talk, but an empty saddle invites questions."

"Let's not worry about the horse right now. You want to take care of him? The body?"

"Yeah, I'll do it. You don't even have to see him."

Gene looked at his own horse. "Maybe I'll get started gettin' my outfit off of Dodger." He shook his head. "That was a good horse."

"Well, he paid for it, the son of a bitch. Let's just be glad he didn't get you." Then he laughed, still nervous but clearly exultant. "You know, I think Charlie was the better shot."

Gene looked at his brother as if he were a stranger. "I think killing is getting easier for you —"

"I don't know. It happened so fast. But I'm sure as hell not sorry. Not in the least bit." Zeke turned cold eyes at Gene. "He would have killed you if he could. You or me, either one."

Gene just said, "I know." Then, "I wish there was something we could do with that dead horse, but I guess it stays where it is."

Zeke looked in Dodger's direction, nodded, and walked away.

It took a little effort, fighting the dead weight, to get the saddle pulled off and out from under the dead horse. Gene shook his head, reflecting how unnecessary it was — all of it. And his own death could have been tossed in, too, just as needlessly and just as meaninglessly. He slipped the bridle off the head, coiled the reins, and hung the bridle on the saddle horn. Then he picked up the saddle and blanket and lugged it all, with the horse smell still fresh on it, back to where he and Zeke last talked.

Zeke was back in about half an hour, leading Bucky. He seemed to be calm about the matter — not strung up and excited, and not rattled or worried. It occurred to Gene that Zeke had been primed for the showdown and he had carried it through — maybe more suddenly than he expected at the actual moment, but he had acted without hesitation. Now he had done the business end of it and was ready for whatever came next.

Gene looked at him. "What say we load my gear onto Bucky and walk back to camp? We can try bunchin' these critters again tomorrow. Let 'em settle down and we'll just start over."

Zeke looked at Gene as if in sympathy. "Are you all right?"

Gene put his hand to his ribs. "I'll be sore, but I'm all right."

"Well, that too, but I meant — well, you don't look good. I'd expect you to be more — relieved, I guess."

Gene heaved a sigh. "Oh, I don't know. Does it end here, or what comes next? We've got a dead horse, a dead man — two dead men, really — and all for what?"

Zeke put a hand on his brother's shoulder. "It's all right. It's over. You're in the clear."

He winked. "Don't worry."

"I told myself I'd stick by you in all of this."

"You did. You have. And you damn near got yourself killed for it. That ought to be enough. From here on out, it'll be easier for the both of us if you stay in the clear."

Gene nodded. "All right," he said. "But I guess I need to know what you did with the body."

"I found a crevice between a couple of big rocks, and I drug him into that. Then I covered him over with a bunch of rocks."

"Do you think you ought to come back up with a shovel and bury him good?"

"I don't know. I'll think about it. I might."

The next morning Gene woke up stiff and sore, and he had a headache. Zeke was already up and had coffee made. He seemed to be in good humor as the two of them sat at the table.

"How are the ribs?"

"A little sore, but I guess I can ride. I imagine we should try bunchin' 'em up again, huh?"

Zeke pursed his lips. "I think I've got a plan, Gene."

"Oh yeah? What's it sound like?"

"I'm a-leavin' Cheyenne."

"Huh?"

"I'm takin' off."

"Today?"

"As good a day as any, if not better. Somebody's goin' to find that horse of his."

"Well, if you hit the trail, that right away puts the blame on you."

"The blame would come my way no matter what. It's mine. This way, I make sure it stays mine."

"Where would you be headed?"

Zeke grinned. "Alaska."

"Alaska? What for?"

"Ain't never been there. It's a long ways away. And that country, at least from what I hear, ain't broke and gelded."

"From what little I've heard, I don't think it's been curried."

"Well, I think that's where I'm a-headed. An' the sooner I head out, the less trouble I'm likely to have with heel flies."

"What about your pay?"

"You think you could send it to me? I got a place in The Dalles where I can probably lay over for a while."

"How much you got comin'?"

"A little over eighty, I'd say."

Gene bit his lip. "I've got that much in my ditty bag. I can give it to you now and get yours from Monte. Maybe you could write a note just to be sure."

"I wasn't expectin' you to do that, Gene."

"I won't be out anything. It's fine with me. And that ought to be easier for you."

"I appreciate it. I really do."

Out of the corner of his eye, Gene thought he saw Zeke bringing his hand up and around to shake. He went to bring his own hand up, as a reflex, until he saw that Zeke had something in his hand. He opened his hand and showed the two elk ivories.

"Give these to your girl," he said.

Gene held his hand open and received them. "Thanks, Zeke."

"That's good luck, from me to her."

"Don't you think you'll need 'em anymore?"

"I got my use out of 'em, I think."

"Well, thanks, Zeke. Sort of a souvenir from the first time you met."

"Sort of. I don't suppose I'll be able to make it for your weddin'."

"Or Rusty George's, either," Gene said, glad to see an opening for a light touch.

Zeke laughed. "No, I imagine I'll miss 'em both."

"It's not goin' to be the same, Zeke."

"Aw, hell, gettin' hitched is gettin' hitched. Happy'll stand up with you."

"No, I mean all of it. With you gone. And not able to come back when you damn well please."

"You got your life to live, Gene. I can see that since I been back. Your trail and mine, they're goin' to come to a fork sooner or later, not a bad one, but your way is bound to be a little tamer than mine. We both see that."

"I'm goin' to miss you, Zeke."

"I'll keep in touch."

"Zeke, I've never known you to write a letter in all your life."

"This isn't it, Gene. We'll see each other again. I just need to vamoose for a while. I'll be in touch, one way or the other. Maybe I'll find me a big fat woman to winter up with, and she'll write you a letter for me."

"There's probably as many women where you're goin' as there is up here on the mountain."

"I'll make out."

"I'm sure you will."

"Well, as soon as we get a bite to eat, I'm thinkin' I'll roll my blankets and rowel out."

Gene smiled and nodded. "Go out north-northwest?"

"Uh-huh. And it wouldn't hurt my feelin's if I found that horse of his on the way out."

After breakfast of bacon and cold biscuits, Gene said, "I need to get word to Monte so he'll send someone up here to give me a hand."

"I'll tell you what," Zeke said. "I'll send him a note from Douglas, tellin' him I've pulled my freight and to give my wages to you. Take care of both those details at once."

Then, without much ceremony Zeke gathered up his gear. As he held out his hand he said, "We'll be seein' you a little farther on down the road."

"All right, Zeke," Gene said huskily. "Be careful."

As Zeke headed Bucky out on the trail that he had taken the morning before, Gene stood at the hitching rail and waved. Zeke waved back and then kicked his horse into a lope. Gene felt tears welling up in his eyes as he thought the words, "Good-bye, my brother."

Zeke left on a Tuesday. On Friday of the next

week, Pete Bonair and Rusty George showed up, with orders for Gene to shag on back to the ranch.

Rusty's first question was about Zeke. "So ol' Zeke got a wild hair and rode with the wind, eh? What got into him?"

Gene shrugged. "Maybe the sound of the choo-choo trains finally got to him."

CHAPTER 17

On the day Gene returned to headquarters, he told Happy what had happened on the mountain. Happy listened to the story without showing much emotion. "Too bad you had to leave that horse just lying there out in the open."

"I could've dragged it someplace, but Dodger would still be a dead horse."

"I guess you're right."

"Well, Zeke thinks this should leave me in the clear."

"Let's hope he's right." Then Happy shook his head. "You know, Gene, I don't think Zeke had to leave."

"He seemed to think so. Or at least he wanted to."

"Yes, but he didn't have to. The details show that Chet opened the fight. You boys would have been in the clear."

"But Zeke went after him, and he'd already made up his mind to kill Chet first if he got a chance. The way things turned out, he got to do what he would have done earlier, and then pulling out would have been the next thing to do."

"That was his style, then, to ride away from

things rather than sort them out and answer to them."

"Yeah, and I think the other part is he didn't want to have to answer for all the Charlie business all over again."

"Then the first cover-up set the pattern for the second one, even though he didn't really need to cover anything the second time."

"Like you say, it was his style."

"And he left you to do the answering."

"He wanted to take this whole thing into his own hands, and I let him. He wanted to bring it on himself and keep me in the clear. But, yeah, I'll probably have some answerin' to do."

"Well, let's hope it works out the way it's supposed to this time."

Gene nodded slowly. Then he said, "You know, Happy, none of this seemed to bother Zeke very much."

"That's the difference between you two. One difference, anyway. But that's not any news to you."

"And you know, Happy, you've got to wonder what Chet was thinkin', if he was thinkin' at all, when he rode right into it like that."

"Probably thought he was on top. Probably didn't have a doubt he was going to win."

"That's the way Zeke was, too. Plumb cocksure he was goin' to win." Gene forced a laugh. "And he did, too." He shook his head. "Zeke said it was like having a big buck deer walk up on him. It reminds me of one fall, when Zeke and I were growing up on the Platte. There was a big buck hung out along the river there — six points on one side and four on the other, and an ass this wide. We hunted him and hunted him, and he always gave us the slip. Then one day, along about midmorning, he and I stumbled into each other, and I shot him just like that. When Zeke and I were sawing off his antlers, half of his brain came along in the skull plate, you know."

Happy nodded.

"So Zeke took a twig to pry out the part of the brain, like you always do, and he said, 'This is the part that wasn't workin' just right today.' That's how it must have been with Chet. He must have been thinkin' about somethin' else for a minute."

"Must have."

"But it's over — that part of it, anyhow. One stupid move on his part, and things take an entirely different course. And if he'd been a better shot, or made a better shot, things would be even different yet."

"I'd say you're lucky to come out of it the way you did. Those boys had bad blood between them."

"Chet and Charlie? Or them and Zeke?"

"All the way around. You got pulled into it, but you got out of it."

"Yeah, as it turned out, they settled it among themselves. They really hated Zeke, and he seemed to have nothing but contempt for them." Gene let out a heavy sigh. "I'm glad it's over, as much as it is. I hope I stay in the clear. I just hope I don't always have it hangin' over me."

"Let's hope so."

Not long after Gene had returned to the bunkhouse, a cold rain moved in to the plains country — a cold, slow, steady rain that turned the roads to gumbo and told of cooler weather on the way. Gene and Tommy Tipton had become partners riding the west range, and they had moved the cattle off the sparse southern range until the next spring. Tommy never asked a question about Zeke or what happened on the mountain, and Gene didn't volunteer any details that might be revealing.

Gene and Happy didn't talk much about it themselves, either. There wasn't much more to talk about — until Sheriff Rolfe came riding in one evening on a spattered horse, dripping rain from his hat, mustache, and slicker.

As was the sheriff's habit, he didn't state his business right away. He sat by the sheet-iron stove and dried out, waiting for supper as the hands drifted in from their day's work. The weather was wet and chilly outside, but the bunkhouse was warm and comfortable. As they came in, the men hung their wet outer clothes on the pegs near the stove, and then sat near to dry off. The sheriff drank coffee and made small talk, having accepted Happy's invitation to stay for supper.

All the way through the evening meal, Gene kept expecting a break in the conversation, a turn that would show the sheriff's purpose. But none came. Gene had the feeling that the sheriff's business was with him, so he stayed at the table as the other hands went back to the sleeping room.

The sheriff brought out his pipe and began the leisurely business of scraping it, filling it, and lighting it. His large mustache smiled over the stem of the pipe, and his clear eyes shone at Gene through the cloud of smoke. Then he asked, "Where's a good place to talk, Gene?"

Gene looked around. "In the kitchen, I suppose."

The sheriff looked at Happy.

"I have no secrets from Happy," Gene said.

"That's fine by me," the sheriff answered. "Shall we?"

When they had gotten seated in the far corner of the small kitchen, and out of Happy's way, the sheriff relit his pipe and bent his gaze upon Gene. "We found a dead man, Gene."

"Oh?"

"Could you guess who it was?"

Gene pursed his lips. "I would guess it was someone you think I knew, or we wouldn't be having this conversation."

"No, we wouldn't. That puts a fence around it." The sheriff puffed. "I understand your brother Zeke left the country, Gene."

"That's correct."

"When did he leave these parts?"

"About a week or so ago."

"And you two were workin' the summer range, on the mountain, when he left?"

"Yes, sir."

"Seems like a nice place to be workin'. Why would Zeke want to leave?"

"I think maybe it was the climate."

"I can imagine. Did he mention what climate he might be seeking as an improvement?"

"I believe he headed north."

The sheriff put a fresh match to his pipe and produced a thick cloud of smoke. "The climate" — he puffed — "*is* cooler up north."

"Getting cool here, too."

"Yes, it is. Yes, it is." The sheriff set his pipe on the small table where they sat. "A few days after your brother left, some Em Tee riders found a horse on their range. It turned out to be a horse belonging to a man you and I both knew."

Gene nodded, showing no expression.

"Between the horse itself and some of the personal effects found on board, it was identified as belonging to Chet Bickford."

"He rode a big sorrel geld," Gene offered.

"Yes, he did. But he seems to have quit riding it at about the time your brother Zeke left the country. I poked around out there for a while, and in a few days, I found the dead man."

Gene detected very little sympathy in the sheriff's tone. "Chet," he confirmed.

"Yes. He seemed to have died from a rifle slug at close range. And do you know where I found him?"

"No. Tell me."

"In a crevice between two large boulders. He had been covered with rocks, but in the warm weather, it was like finding a billy goat in the dark."

"I see."

"And where do you think this was, Gene?"

"I wouldn't know for sure."

"It was about a quarter of a mile, through some timber, from the spot where I found a dead horse. Your horse, Dodger."

"How did you know it was Dodger?"

"Your *compadres* Pete and Rusty told me that much. But they didn't seem to know anything about Chet."

"Dodger was a good horse," Gene said.

"When did he die?"

"Shortly before Zeke left."

The sheriff nodded. "I wouldn't want to ask you a question you might feel tempted to lie about, Gene." He took up his pipe and relit it. "So tell me, Gene. When did you last see Chet Bickford?"

"It was in early July or so, around the tenth or fifteenth. About a month before Zeke left."

"You didn't see him since that?"

"No, sir."

"How did it happen you saw him when you did?"

"He stopped in at our cow camp and bummed a meal," Gene said, not unaware of the possible flinch he might cause.

"That's odd," said the sheriff. "What seemed to have taken him up to that country?"

"He said he was hunting mountain lions."

The sheriff arched his eyebrows. "How long did he stay around?"

"Just for supper. He didn't even spend the night, but of course we invited him to."

"I see." The sheriff took a long, studied look at the burnt embers in his pipe. Then he spoke. "It's my opinion, Gene, that a crime was committed up there. A man was killed by another man. I am going to file a warrant for Ezekiel Hill for the murder of Chester Bickford. Circumstances justify my doing so, what with Zeke leaving at the time he did."

"I understand."

"Chet was unhappy about his brother's death," the sheriff said. "I know he suspected your brother, but there wasn't any direct evidence. But in this case, I have enough evidence and enough coincidence to seek a warrant. You understand all of this?"

"Yes, I do."

"Maybe Zeke killed a man. Maybe it was self-defense. And maybe it will be determined if he ever comes back to this country." The sheriff put his pipe into his pocket. "Do you have any questions, Gene?"

"None at all."

"Well enough, then. I think I'll go back to town." He thanked Happy on the way out, then he was gone.

Happy gave an inquiring look at Gene, who asked, "Did you follow that?"

"Just about every word. In the eyes of the law,

it looks like you're in the clear."

Gene nodded. But they both knew, without saying it, that Gene still had to answer to his own conscience. And he hadn't yet seen Katharine since he had come back from the mountain. . . .

CHAPTER 18

Sheriff Rolfe had visited on a Friday. On Saturday night, Gene stayed at the bunkhouse while the other hands went for a night in town. Gene, who was not that much of a nightlifer anyway, wanted to be well rested and clear-headed for his Sunday visit to Katharine.

The cold weather that had drenched the sheriff had not yet passed over. Gene and Happy spent the evening by the stove, talking lightly about this topic and that, enjoying the quiet and calm of the night. At about ten o'clock Gene went out to use the privy, and when he came back in, a stranger was sitting in a third chair drawn up to the stove.

"Well, here's Pokey now," Happy said loud.

Gene perked up. Pokey had been his nickname when he and Zeke were boys, but no one had called him that since their parents had died. Happy knew of the childhood nickname, and he probably was using it now as a cover. That meant the stranger might be here on sinister business.

In the instant between being announced and having the man introduced, Gene took a full look at the stranger. The face carried some traces of familiarity, but nothing readily identified. A week's stubble of salt-and-pepper beard covered the lower half of the face, while the upper half was flushed in the dull, dark, mottled plum color of a face ravaged by hard living. The skin was coarse and puffy and pocked, shot through and through with broken blood vessels across the nose and upper cheeks. The eyes were a muddy brown, with the whites no longer white but a filmy yellow that looked both jaundiced and rheumy. The man was at least in his mid-fifties, but his was an old face for a man of that age. It wore the badge of reckless living, with ill feelings etched in it.

Gene was trying to associate the features when Happy said, "Pokey, this is Jess Bickford. Jess, this is Pokey, the one cowhand who had the brains to stay home on a night like this."

A chill ran through Gene. This would be a father or an uncle.

The man, who seemed to be not yet warm enough to take off his hat and coat, sat hunched by the stove, out of the full glow of the lamplight. Without rising from his chair he held out a weathered hand and, shaking Gene's briefly, said "Pleased t'meet ya."

Gene returned the compliment with equal sincerity and sat down. He was conscious of a raw power in the man, just as he had felt it in Chet and Charlie, especially when they were riled in Zeke's presence.

Happy said, not cheerfully, but in a solemn tone that seemed to speak respect for the dead, "Jess is Chet and Charlie's father."

"Oh," said Gene. He didn't say he was sorry, for he had learned his lesson with that phrase. Instead he just took another look at the father. The man seemed to emanate evil, as if whatever had been bad in the sons originated in him, distilled, and been passed on to them in diluted form.

Gene decided to assume the role of the cowhand who didn't speak much. He moved his chair back from the stove.

Happy drew out his pipe and loaded it with tobacco. He lit it, tamped it, and lit it again. Blowing out a rich cloud of smoke, he said, "Weather turned rather unfriendly on us here. Are you passing through, Mr. Bickford, or are you staying in the area?"

"No need to mister me. I been around for a little while, and I aim to move on."

"You're certainly welcome to stay a night here," said Happy, with no apparent enthusiasm.

"Thanks, but I already have me a camp. I just come here to check on what I've heard."

Happy laid his palm over his pipe and puffed twice with purpose. "Lots of things to be heard, I would think."

Jess shivered. "My God, but this is a cold, miserable country! I'm glad I'm not stayin'."

"First time for you here?"

"No. Hell, no. I been here before and I didn't like it then, either!" Jess drew a pint bottle of whiskey from inside his coat, uncapped it, and took a swallow. He offered it to the other two, who both declined. Then he took another swallow, faintly smacked his lips and stretched them over his teeth, and shook his head as he grimaced.

"Then you're probably not here on a pleasure trip," suggested Happy.

"No, I'm not. Not by a damn sight. I'm here on business." He glared at each of them. "I'm not makin' a secret of it." His face clouded up and his upper lip trembled, and then his ill humor regained control. "I lost two sons here. I know one was killed and I got a damn good hunch the other one was too. And the little son of a bitch I want to hold accountable for it has skipped the country."

Happy raised his eyebrows and puffed his pipe. "Since there are no secrets, I presume you mean Zeke Hill."

"That's exactly who I mean!" The older man's anger flared, and he spit as he talked. He took another drink and it seemed to calm him. A smug look of self-satisfaction spread over him as he licked his lips with the tip of his tongue. Gloating now like Charlie in his prime, he said, "I'm gonna catch that little son of a bitch and I'm gonna poke my gun barrel in his snoot."

"Do you know Zeke?" asked Happy.

"I know him when I see him. But he don't know me."

Jess went to take another drink and then paused. "And I'll tell you somethin' else. I'm gonna blow his brains out!" Then he took his drink, licked his lips, and nodded his head. He had quit shivering by now, and he took off his hat, to show a full head of black hair streaked with silver. Drawing out a pouch of tobacco, he rolled a cigarette, deftly. As he fashioned the smoke he breathed through his open mouth. Gene noticed the yellowed teeth — the upper front teeth were straight and narrow with a gap between them.

Jess seemed to be warm and relaxed now, between the outer warmth of the stove and the inner fire of the whiskey. He was sitting up straight. "Yep. That's what I'm gonna do. I'm gonna shove my gun barrel in his face and tell him how the cow ate the cabbage. Then I'll pull the trigger." He lit the cigarette. "He killed my boys. They was all I had. Do you blame me? Huh?"

Happy shook his head.

Gene shook his head.

"I hate him more than anyone on the face of this earth."

Happy struck a match and paused with it over his pipe. "Zeke is probably a long ways from here by now. He's been gone a couple of months."

"If he ever comes back to this country, I'll hear word — and I'll be back." Jess nodded. "I'll get him." He slumped again, back into a hunch. He sat there quietly smoking for several minutes, his lips moving as if he were mouthing words but not giving them utterance.

Gene looked at the bottle and at the man. He had taken a pretty good dose of whiskey in a short while.

Happy must have been thinking along the same lines. "I'm not going to tell another man his business," he said, "but you might want to sleep inside tonight."

Jess looked at the two of them as if they might murder him in his sleep and he was too smart for them. "Nope. I'll ride back to my camp. Anyone comes around it, by God, and they'll find out what-for."

"I don't think you have to worry about anybody bothering you," said Happy.

"I ain't worried." His head bobbed lightly. "Not me." He stood up, swaying until he steadied.

Gene took his measure. He was as tall as his two boys but not quite as burly. Gene looked at the boots. They were worn on the outsides, heels and soles, like Chet and Charlie's boots, only more pronounced.

"Don't be in any hurry to leave," Happy said, without much urging in his voice.

"I got some country to cover," said Jess, and he walked out the door.

They could barely hear the hoofbeats on the wet ground, but when they were sure he was gone, Happy said, "That was very interesting."

"It sure was," said Gene. "I hope he makes it back to Texas and stays there."

Happy opened the stove lid to spit inside. The fire glowed against his pale hair as he said, "I hope so, too."

On Sunday, Gene bathed and shaved and put on a fresh shirt. He saddled his new good horse, Tugger, and rode to the Rose homestead. The cold storm had passed over, and the sun was warm on his back as he rode. The prairie, which had been parched, seemed refreshed by the rain. Life was still young and full of promise, but it was not innocent. There were some things he could not undo, but he could make them better with the person he was going to see.

Katharine was brushing Molly the dun mare when he rode up. They had apparently been on a ride before the day warmed up in earnest. The horse had a saddle of drying sweat on its back.

The butterfly in Gene's stomach flapped in its familiar way when he saw her. She saw him and waved, and in the motion as he waved back it seemed as if their spirits fluttered out to meet. Yes, he was sure of it. They could go on from here.

"I see you're back," she said as he dismounted.

"That's right. Zeke decided to move on down the trail, so Monte had me come back while he sent Pete and Rusty to take over for us."

"I heard Zeke was gone." She slapped the knot of the lead rope in her hand.

"Did you hear anything else?"

"No, just that he was gone."

"There's a little more to the story than that." Gene loosened his cinch.

"I thought there might be."

"If you want to put your horse away, I can tie mine up and tell you about it."

Her eyes danced as always with her smile. "Is it a long story?"

"Medium." He half-smiled and half-frowned.

"Then why don't you turn your horse into the corral and stay awhile?"

He took her right hand in his left, pressed it to his lips, and said, "Sure."

Once under their favorite cottonwood tree, they embraced for a long moment. Then he looked into her eyes, and he could tell that the current was flowing between them as always. It hadn't been spoiled.

"Is it bad?" she asked.

"Let's sit down." They sat as before, at a right angle to one another, knees almost touching and hands overlaid. He took a deep breath and began. "Chet came after us the day you and Happy left. That afternoon. It was up in that same pasture where I met up with you two."

"Uh-huh."

"He shot at me from the back, but he didn't make a good shot."

She squeezed his hand.

"The bullet cut through my shirt, scraped my ribs, and got my horse Dodger in the neck. I bailed off and got into the timber, and in the shooting he hit the horse again and then finished him off."

Her face had a pained look of fear and sorrow. "So your good horse Dodger is gone."

He nodded. "Plumb gone. Then Zeke came around and found me. I was goin' to keep Chet's attention with a shot every ten minutes or so, and Zeke was goin' to sneak up around and in back of him, and get to him that way. Chet was up

217

in the rocks. Zeke was gone less than ten minutes, and all of a sudden I hear a shot, and Zeke comes back sayin' Charlie — I mean Chet — came ridin' right down to him, and Zeke shot him, just like that."

"And that's why Zeke left."

"Right. He covered up the body, he said, in a crevice. Put some rocks over it."

"Oh, Gene —"

"Zeke took it all onto himself. He killed Chet in self-defense. Then he told me if I didn't see anything or have a hand in anything, it would be easier for me to stay in the clear."

She nodded. "That makes sense."

"So the next day, he pulled out. He figured if he left right away he'd have a good chance of gettin' out of the country, and he'd get the blame for it, which he was willin' to do."

Her eyes met his. "That makes it hard on him, but it seems fair."

"If he ever comes back to this country he'll have some answerin' to do."

"Where was he headed, or should I ask?"

"Alaska."

Her eyes widened. "That's like another country."

"Almost."

She pressed his hand. "You're going to miss him, aren't you?"

"Yes, I am." Then he leaned and quick-kissed her. "But I have you."

"Yes," she said. "You have me. And I have you.

But in a way, I can tell from the way you're telling me, you feel that you're losing a brother."

"Oh, I know I'll see him again. But as he said, our trails were goin' to branch off sooner or later. We both could see we were headed like that."

"Still, he's your only family."

"Not for long, I hope." And they kissed again.

"It's like in the Bible," she said, "the part they read at a wedding. It says that a woman leaves her parents to start a new family, and the man does the same thing."

Gene nodded. "I've heard them say that. It means you give up one family to start another."

"Not all the way. You don't have to give them up all the way."

"Right. But the new family comes first." He thought for a long moment, and he felt washed over by a strong realization. He felt dreamy as he looked at her.

"What is it, Gene?"

"An idea just came together for me, something I'd been thinking about — sort of in pieces, I guess."

"Go ahead."

"This is goin' to sound crazy."

"No it isn't." Her eyes were shining as she nodded encouragement.

"There were times when we were growin' up that Zeke and I were like the same person. It was as if there were places where we just ran together into one person, not one of us stopping at a point where the other started. Do I make sense?"

"I think so."

219

"Then, when he came back from Texas, it seemed like he was all the time separate from me now. Everything in his head was just in his head, and everything in mine was just in mine. We were different. And sometimes, especially in this business with Chet and Charlie, he seemed like a stranger to me. This sounds crazy, doesn't it?"

"No, it doesn't. Go on."

"Well, maybe what I mean to say is, he's still my brother, but I don't feel like we're really part of each other anymore."

Katharine nodded solemnly and pressed his hand.

Then he brightened. "But you and I are."

"We . . ."

"We've grown into one another, like we're a part of each other now. That's the rest of the idea that just came to me. Zeke and I grew apart, while you and I grew together . . . into two people that are . . . one whole person."

"I know what you mean. Sometimes I feel that, too, like when we were standing here a few minutes ago. It was like there was no beginning or ending."

"That probably goes along with what the Bible says."

She smiled. "It seems to fit just right."

They didn't speak for a moment, and then an image flashed in his memory. "I almost forgot," he said, digging into his pocket. "Zeke asked me to give you these." He held out the pair of elk ivories.

Her eyes softened as she took the tokens. "That

was very thoughtful of him." She paused and then said, "In a way I get a brother in the deal, don't I?"

"I think he meant it that way."

Gene stood there with his partner and his equal, and he was free to ride with her, stirrup to stirrup, down life's trail. It would be the two of them, now.

Then he thought of Zeke, nonchalant and undaunted, maybe in Alaska by now, dealing his favorite seven-card-stud game among the gold miners and salmon fishermen. Whenever Gene imagined Zeke's face it had a smile on it. After all that had happened, Gene knew he would always remember his brother as he was that spring day on the prairie — dancing in the saddle, vaulting clear, and landing in a perfect walk — Zeke wearing a white hat and red shirt and riding Bucky, the day he came home from Texas.